THAT HEX FACTOR

M.J. CAAN

BOOKS

By M.J. Caan

Singing Falls Witches

Hex After Forty
That Good Hex
How Torie Got Her Hex Back
Hex and Chocolate
Moonlight Hexes
Hex and the Single Witch
Hex Education
Hex After Dark
That Hex Factor

Vinci Books

vinci-books.com

Published by Vinci Books Ltd in 2025

1

A CIP catalogue record for this book is available from the British Library.
Paperback ISBN: 9781036705657
The EU GPSR authorised representative is Logos Europe, 9 rue Nicolas
Poussion, 17000 La Rochelle, France contact@logoseurope.eu

Chapter One

Torie bolted upright in bed, her hand on her throat, a scream locked in her chest. She was covered in sweat, the pounding of her heart so loud in her ears that she was certain it could be heard throughout the house.

Squeezing her eyes shut, she slammed a fist into the mattress, telling herself it wasn't real, that it was just a dream. No matter how real it felt at the time, it was only a dream.

Of course, it didn't help that it was the same one she had experienced constantly over the last few nights.

It started off pleasant enough, with her walking the grounds of a beautiful Federal-style house, with lovely gardens overlooking a large pond. But without fail, as she walked, everything around her would begin to morph into something unrecognizable. The white siding of the house would melt and puddle like ice cream sliding down a cone on a sunny day. The flowers in the garden wilted, their petals dropping to become pock marks on the browning grass.

That's when she would turn and run, fear telling her not to look back, but to keep driving her legs forward to get away from what was to come. Only she couldn't run. The ground beneath her became soft and soggy, pulling her in to her knees. She would reach upward to the heavens, screaming for someone to pull her free, only to have the earth reach up with dark tentacles made of sticky tar and wrap themselves around her, pulling her backwards and deeper into the ground.

She would open her mouth to scream, only to have it fill with dirt as she was swallowed whole. She would awaken, gulping air and clutching at her chest, lost in the haze of her nightmare.

In the darkness of the room, she felt a comforting, warm buzzing in her lap. The iridescent display of lights playing along Leo's scales helped to ground her. The soft vibration passing through his body, and the soft, loving emerald glow of his eyes told Torie she is safe in this space.

Letting out a deep breath, she stroked Leo's back, luxuriating in the tranquility he radiated.

"My little therapy dragon," she said quietly into the darkness. Reaching to her side, she felt the empty space where Elric had been. She smiled down at Leo. "Oh well, I guess somebody got tired of being awakened by my night terrors." She leaned forward, snuggling her face against the dragon's snout. "But not you. Not mama's little baby."

Once he was content everything was alright, Leo hopped off the bed and made his way back to the little cushion he had adopted as his bed, and curled back up, tiny wisps of smoke exiting his nostrils as he fell almost immediately back into a deep sleep.

Torie tossed about, flipping her pillow to the cooler side,

and finally drifted off for a bit, knowing that dawn was only hours away.

Light pouring in through the windows came all too swiftly, and she dragged herself from the bed, threw on a robe, and followed her nose to the kitchen. The smell of freshly brewed coffee, bacon, eggs, and the sweet scent of cinnamon and maple that hinted at French toast all but made her salivate.

"Good morning," she said to Elric, as she made her way to the doors to let Leo out. She left it open for him to return once he was done with his business and moved to stand next to Elric at the stove, stretching onto her tip-toes to give him a quick kiss. "Did I wake you up last night?"

The big wolf shook his head while flipping a piece of toast. "Not at all. I couldn't sleep so I went for a run. Full moon is drawing close."

Torie nodded. She was usually pretty good about keeping up with the cycles of the moon, knowing how it could affect werewolves, but lately she was more wrapped up in what was going on in her own mind.

"Why do you ask?" Elric said. "More of those dreams?"

She nodded, moving over to the island where she grabbed a piece of bacon to crunch on. "It's so weird. It's the same one. The details never change."

Elric turned off the range and spun around to face her, holding a plate of French toast in one hand and a tray of eggs in the other. He made his way to the island just as the cupboards opened and a couple of plates flew from them to settle gracefully in front of Torie.

"There's fresh squeezed orange juice in the fridge," he

said, nodding at the gleaming silver Sub-Zero that hulked along one wall.

Torie grabbed the OJ and returned, staring at all the food. "Is someone coming over I don't know about? You made enough for a family get together." She saw him arch a single eyebrow and couldn't help but break into a smile. "Or a witch, a hungry werewolf and a bottomless pit masquerading as a baby dragon."

Elric laughed, taking a seat beside her as they both began loading their plates. The wolf smiled, leaning over and giving a few slabs of bacon to a patiently waiting Leo, before addressing Torie. "You know, I really think you need to talk to someone about these nightmares. I don't know who...but isn't there some kind of hotline or therapist you can reach out to?"

Torie gave him a weak grin and shook her head. "No, not quite. You're the closest thing I have to that. Well, and Jasmin of course. And she is already buried in research trying to figure out what they mean."

The mention of her best friend, and fellow witch, made her briefly wonder where Jasmin was. It wasn't like her not to show up for breakfast, especially after Torie had let her know French toast was on the menu.

Elric cleared his throat. "I mean, it's pretty obvious what's going on."

Torie raised her eyebrows and set down her cup of juice. "Oh? Do tell."

He swallowed a mouthful of golden toast, dabbing at a drop of maple syrup on his lips. "Torie, you were kidnapped and locked in a bottle, sealed away from everything. You almost died, my dear. It doesn't take a psychoanalyst to connect the dots. In your dreams, the earth is swallowing you whole, trapping you. You are reliving your trauma."

Torie smiled, giving her boyfriend her complete atten-tion. "Is that your professional opinion?"

"I'm a wolf. In my opinion, the simplest explanation is usually the right one."

Torie sighed, pushing the plate in front of her away. "I wish it were that simple. But this feels so different. It's so real. And while it's hard to explain, it feels like it is getting more real each night." She shook her head and took her plate with leftovers on it and sat it on the floor in front of Leo. She held up one finger in admonishment. "And no charring the food. You've burned up enough of my plates doing that."

The little dragon murmured something deep from his chest as he buried his face happily in the plate.

"I think he just talked back to you," said Elric.

Torie laughed. "It's like he's hitting his terrible-twos or something." Despite his sometimes-sassy demeanor, she couldn't help but be filled with love every time she looked at Leo.

"You know, he's growing fast," said Elric. His tone was more leading than just making a statement.

"I know. But he's still just a little thing."

"Yes, but he's a dragon. Who knows how long he'll be little?"

She knew what he was saying. It wasn't anything she hadn't heard from Jasmin before. And truthfully it had occurred to her as well. But she pushed such thoughts to the back of her mind.

"I don't care how big he gets. He's my family now."

Elric smiled, looking from Torie to the dragon that was literally licking his plate clean. "That's true. He's saved you a couple of times now. I guess he's not going anywhere." He stood up and began clearing the island and loading the dishwasher.

"You know, the house will do that for you," Torie said.

He shrugged. "I know. But I kind of like doing it myself. When the house does it, there's something creepy about it."

Torie folded her arms. "Are you saying my magic creeps you out?"

Elric gave her one of his lopsided grins and wrapped his arms around her. "Your magic is the farthest thing from creepy. I love it when you hex me." Torie threw her head back in laughter. "But when I get out of the shower and there's a towel floating in the air waiting for me? Creepy."

"Okay, I'll give you that," said Torie. "But you'll get used to it."

Elric let out a playful groan. "That's what I'm afraid of." He pulled away and resumed his cleaning. "So, what's on tap for today?"

"I'm meeting Jasmin at the bakery this morning. We are going to go over everything we've been able to learn about Rowena Blackwood, which isn't much at all, and what we've learned about the supernatural community in Salem, before we head up there."

Elric didn't say anything, but Torie could see the tension creep into his frame. The muscles in his back strained at the tee shirt he wore as he increased the speed with which he scrubbed the range top.

"We have to do this, Elric."

He sighed, his head dropping. "I know. Really, I do. But that doesn't mean I have to like it. And I'd feel better if I were by your side when you go."

"And I appreciate that. Truth be told I'd probably feel a lot better knowing you were with me. But we agreed it was better that you stayed here."

He half turned his head in her direction. "Did we though?"

She smiled. "Well, we agreed in principal. With everything happening, I know Max will be more comfortable with you here to back him up. It feels like we are being hit on multiple fronts here. He trusts you, and right now he needs you at his side."

Elric didn't say anything, only nodding as he continued his assault on the Viking range. Torie was right of course. In a town that was comprised of a lot of supernatural creatures, the sheriff would need all the help he could get if something dark was afoot.

And there was something very dark in the works.

"Just...promise you'll be careful. You don't know who or what this Rowena person is. Don't take any chances."

"No chances. I promise." She loved the way he longed to protect her. In the beginning of their relationship, she had been somewhat taken aback, thinking that he didn't believe she was capable of taking care of herself. That she needed a man to always protect her. But now, she realized that his actions weren't driven from his own desire to control her, or by any outdated machismo ideals.

No. He loved her. Pure and simple. And he would do anything in the world to keep her safe. And there was a truth and a warmth in that purity that she had never known before.

"I'm going for a run," Elric said. He gave the stove one last glance before disposing of the wipe in the trash.

Torie nodded. "Are you okay?"

He gave her a genuine smile. "I am. Promise. I just have a lot of excess energy this close to a full moon. Need to burn a little more."

"Okay. Now it's my turn to tell you to be careful out

there." She gave him a peck on the lips as he headed for the back door. "I'll see you later this evening and let you know what we come up with."

"Sounds good," he said, then disappeared out the door and across the patio.

Torie watched as he disappeared, leaping over the iron fence and dropping out of view.

She took a deep breath and steeled herself for what was to come. With a sigh, she made her way back to the bedroom. She had just enough time for a shower before meeting Jasmin and Fionna at the bakery the three of them had purchased. Instinctively, she reached out with her mind, feeling for the protective wards around the house, strengthening them with a whisper. The memory of her nightmare clawed its way into her mind once again, and she shivered.

Something was coming. She could feel it deep inside. And no matter how much magic she poured into the wards around her, she wasn't certain she would be able to keep it out.

Chapter Two

As Torie pushed open the door to the Brew Cup Bakery, the charming, tinkling melody of the door chime set the tone for a cozy and welcoming atmosphere. Fionna had truly outdone herself on the decor, and both Torie and Jasmin couldn't have been prouder of her choices.

The bakery was bathed in warm, amber light emanating from antique brass fixtures hanging from the ceiling. The walls were adorned with vintage, floral-patterned wallpaper and lined with wooden shelves housing an assortment of antique pans and kitchenware from years gone by.

The aroma of freshly baked goods enveloped Torie, a tantalizing blend of buttery croissants, rich chocolate, and the faintest hint of cinnamon and fresh berries. Even though she had just eaten, the scent was intoxicating and stirred her hunger. As she inhaled deeply, she could almost taste the sugary sweetness of the raspberry-filled Danishes and the flaky, buttery layers of the golden-brown Palmiers.

It was early morning, but the place was already quite busy. A soft jazz tune played in the background, melding with the pleasant hum of conversation from the humans gathered around the mismatched antique tables, sipping on steaming mugs of coffee and tea. The gentle clinking of porcelain and silverware, coupled with the sound of laughter, created a welcoming atmosphere of comfort and belonging.

However, it was the subtle details Fionna had added that truly made Brew Cup Bakery a haven for supernaturals. Upon closer inspection, the intricate wallpaper pattern revealed tiny crescent moons and stars hidden amidst the flowers—a symbol of the safe space this bakery provided. An ethereal glow, perceptible only to supernatural beings, emanated from a beautifully crafted stained-glass window featuring a waning moon and an array of mythical creatures dancing in the night sky.

A faint, but noticeable, scent of sage and lavender lingered in the air, the remnants of a protection spell woven by Torie and Jasmin that was meant to safeguard any supernaturals who sought refuge within the bakery's walls. The spell, undetectable to humans, provided a sense of security and peace for the magical patrons.

Behind the glass display case, Fionna stood with Tara, one of her new employees. She whispered conspiratorially to the young girl, who giggled in response. Fionna looked up to Torie as she entered, giving her a nod and an inviting smile. She was dressed in jeans and a sleeveless tee shirt that showed off her toned arms. The only jewelry, other than her wedding band, was a silver pendant with an intricate tree of life design resting on her chest.

"Well, hey there," she said, her voice warm and soothing, like a cup of hot cocoa on a cold winter's night. "Grab our seats. I'll be over in a second."

As Torie stepped farther into the enchanting bakery, she

couldn't help but feel a sense of belonging wash over her. Here, she was not just another customer. She was not just an owner. She was part of a secret world where the magical and the mundane intertwined; a harmonious symphony that celebrated the extraordinary.

Torie made her way to the enormous fireplace dominating the back of the cafe. There was a table with three high-backed leather chairs that sat facing the hearth.

Their chairs.

Despite the fact that the cafe had no reservation system in place, no matter how busy it was, these seats were always open. It was as if everyone just knew who that space belonged to.

Torie approached the chairs and was happy to see Jasmin already seated, discreet jewelry sparkling against her yellow sundress, her afro a glorious halo of a cloud.

"There you are," said Torie. "I missed you at breakfast this morning."

"Oh. Was it French toast?" Just the tiniest pang of longing in her voice.

Torie nodded. "And the extra-crispy bacon."

Jasmin shook her head and let out a sigh. "Girl, you know I can't be eating like that anymore. I'm at a point where all that salt is not good for me. And all that sugar goes right to my hips and stays there." She gave Torie a playful up and down look. "But it seems like having a wolf full time in residence is agreeing with you. How are you staying so fit?"

Torie rolled her eyes. "It's because that man loves to work out. And he makes me do it with him most of the time."

Jasmin's eyes narrowed and her brows danced comically. "Oh, I bet he does."

Torie laughed and playfully slapped at her friend's arm just as Fionna approached with a tray laden with two French presses and a tray of fresh baked scones.

"What's so funny?" she asked.

"Just laughing at how good Elric has been for Torie," said Jasmin. "She's been getting her workouts in."

Fionna joined in the laughter. "You two are great together. Isn't it about time you make it official?"

Torie rolled her eyes again, waving Fionna off. Then she noticed Jasmin wasn't saying anything, and instead was pouring herself a cup of coffee.

"Jas – why did you suddenly go radio silent?" Torie said, squinting at her friend.

Jasmin looked at her, eyes wide. "What? Nothing. Unlike some people, I haven't eaten all morning and have been looking forward to diving into these scones. Is that alright?" She returned to fixing her coffee and making a point of shoveling a big bite of her scone into her mouth.

"Uh-huh," said Torie, reaching for a cup while side-eyeing her friend.

Fionna dropped into the third chair and reached for a scone. "Well, did you two decide what you're going to do about the whole Salem thing? Are you waiting it out or paying that Rowena person a visit?"

Torie nervously gnawed on her bottom lip; her eyes wide as she contemplated. "We have to go to her," she said hesitantly.

Jasmin nodded, her expression solemn and serious. "Yes. We've tried a variety of revelation spells as well as communication and location ones. All to no avail. So, all that's left is an in-person visit."

Fionna nodded, taking a small nibble of her scone. "When are you leaving?"

"Tomorrow," said Jasmin. "And there's still plenty of seats left on the plane if you want to join us."

They had asked Fionna before and knew her answer had most likely not changed.

Fionna looked down, her leg bouncing with anxious energy. "You guys know I have your back no matter what, right? But shifters and planes don't mix. Especially not me. I mean, we're meant to be close to the ground, not soaring so far above it. Just the thought of being so far removed from the earth...it's just not natural. I'm breaking out in a cold sweat just thinking about it."

Torie reached out, placing a protective hand on her friend's knee. "You don't have to explain yourself. Ever. We wouldn't have asked a second time, but just wanted to make sure you hadn't changed your mind."

Fionna smiled and covered Torie's hand with her own.

"Well, I guess the good thing is, someone will be here to keep this place running. You really have done amazing things here," said Jasmin.

"Agreed," added Torie. "It's more than I could have ever imagined."

Fionna beamed with pride. "Well, now all we have to do is keep it from being destroyed by malignant forces or more bodies showing up here."

Jasmin cleared her throat. "And that's why we are going to Salem. Whatever Eliza's old coven may know could help us to figure out what's going on here. Before it's too late."

Torie shuddered at her friend's words.

Jasmin gave her a concerned look. "What is it?"

Torie sighed, sipping her coffee. "More bad dreams. Can't seem to shake them."

"Did you try the herbal tea I gave you?" asked Jasmin.

She nodded, letting out another sigh. "I did. Didn't help.

All it made me do was wake up from my nightmares needing to go to the bathroom really bad."

Fionna swallowed a bite of scone. "It's probably because you were stuck in that bottle. You're just reliving that." She stopped mid-chew as Torie gave her a look. "What?"

Torie was shaking her head. "Must be a shifter thing."

"Huh?" said Fionna, her confusion not interfering with her enjoyment of the scone.

"Never mind," said Torie. "Let's just say you aren't the first to tell me that." Torie frowned as she watched Fionna finish off the scone and reach for another. "Looks like Jasmin wasn't the only one who didn't eat this morning."

Fionna stopped chewing and stared at the pastry in her hand. "Wow. I didn't even realize I had grabbed another one. I think that's like the tenth thing I've eaten today. I can't seem to stop." She laughed politely and placed the scone on her napkin, sitting it back on the tray.

"Hey, if I were blessed with your metabolism, I'd eat like that too," said Jasmin.

Fionna shifted her weight in her seat, looking around the cafe. "Well, it's getting a bit busier. I need to go help the runner getting orders out. You'll give me a call before you board the plane, yes?"

"Of course," said Torie, standing up. "We'll let you know when we land as well."

They said their goodbyes with a quick embrace and watched as Fionna scooted off to disappear behind the glass counter and through the swinging metal doors that led to the bakery's kitchen.

"Did she seem okay to you?" Jasmin asked.

"I was just about to ask you the same thing."

They gathered their dishes and took them to the receptacle, scraping them into the bin and placing the tray and plate back on top before heading out into the sunlight.

Torie basked in the brightness of the day, tilting her head back to bathe in the golden rays. "How can everything be so beautiful on the outside, and so festering on the inside?" She looked down Main Street, watching the bustling foot traffic as people wandered in and out of the shops that lined the busy street. "Wow. It's busy everywhere today. Are there sales or something we don't know about?"

"Well, I did hear that the hardware store is having a buy two lightbulbs, get the third for free sale," said Jasmin.

Torie smiled. "We're lucky to live here, you know that."

Jasmin hooked her arm in Torie's as they headed down the street. "And that's why we are going to make sure nothing happens to Singing Falls."

They made their way a half-block down the street, heading for their cars. As they passed the tea shop, a man barreled into them as he rushed out the door.

"Oh, excuse me," said Torie instinctively, latching onto Jasmin's arm for support in order to keep from toppling over.

"What?" said the man, adjusting a set of eyeglasses and looking around nervously. "Yes, you need to be excused. You're in my way."

Jasmin narrowed her eyes. "Hey, just a minute. You ran into us. Almost knocked us down."

The man shuffled in place, his eyes darting around nervously. "Of course. You're right. Entirely my fault. I...I don't know why I was in such a hurry."

Torie opened her mouth to say that it was alright, but before she could, the man's face changed. It was quick, and she barely noticed it, but his face narrowed, his nose elongated briefly, and his two front teeth became very pronounced. He opened his mouth and barked a high-pitched squeal at the women, causing them both to jump back.

Then, just as quickly as it happened, his face was back to normal. Shock and embarrassment flooded his features as a hand shot to his mouth. His eyes were wide in disbelief and all he could do was shake his head as he turned and rushed away from the witches.

"What in the world was that about?" asked Jasmin.

Torie narrowed her eyes, watching as the man receded from them. "No idea. But the sooner we find this Rowena woman and find out what she knows, the better I'll feel about things."

Chapter Three

Espresso.

That was what the morning called for. Torie was up at first light, waiting for the fancy, wall-unit coffee maker that no one in the house used, to finally chug out a tiny cup of condensed caffeine. It was just enough to shake off her residual drowsiness after yet another sleepless night.

Again, she had awakened to an empty bed, with only a concerned Leo to snuggle up to. Just as she drained the last drop of non-magical elixir from the cup, Elric walked in through the back doors, breathing heavily and soaked in sweat.

"Good morning," he said. "I went for another run. Couldn't sleep."

"Oh, okay. Well, are you still able to run me and Jasmin to the airport this morning?"

Elric looked at his watch, eyes wide. "Give me fifteen minutes to shower and change." He rushed off, and Torie could hear him loping up the stairs two at a time.

She shook her head and texted Jasmin, letting her know

they would swing by her house in thirty minutes to head to the airport.

Twenty minutes later, she was sitting in the living room, her travel bag next to her, tapping her foot as she waited for Elric. Finally, she went upstairs to find the wolf standing before the full-length mirror, running a comb through his hair, his eyes fixated on his reflection.

"Elric? What's going on? Are you coming down?"

The wolf looked at her absentmindedly. "Oh yeah...sorry." He started to follow her out of the bedroom, but she stopped him, looking down. He followed her gaze then grinned sheepishly as he realized he was only wearing a pair of boxers. "Oh! Sorry. I guess not sleeping is having an effect on me as well."

Grabbing his pants off the chair, along with a button-up shirt, he began pulling on his clothes while making his way towards the stairs.

"You sure you're okay?" Torie asked as they climbed into the car.

"Of course," he replied, climbing behind the wheel. "The moon phase will pass soon, and things will be back to normal. At least for another month."

They drove down the private road to the next driveway where Jasmin was waiting. Elric got out and loaded her suitcase in, squeezing it next to Torie's.

In minutes they were on their way, the big SUV easing out onto the winding mountainside roads that would take them to the regional airport nearly an hour away.

"Do you have everything we will need?" Torie asked, looking over her shoulder to her best friend.

"I think so. We've had no luck finding Rowena from here, but I'm hoping that if we're in the same town as she is, we should be able to find her with a divination spell. All we need to buy is a map of the area once we are there, and then we can use the divining crystals. I have to try and get a fix on her."

"And if that doesn't work?" Torie asked.

Jasmin's voice dropped. "Well, in that case, I have another, more direct method that might work."

Elric's eyes flitted to the rearview mirror briefly before settling back on the road. "I don't like the sound of that."

"Look, we don't have any idea what this Rowena woman is. We don't know for sure that we'll be able to locate her with magic, even if we are in her immediate vicinity. So, if we can't find her, then the next best thing..."

"Is to make her come to us," said Torie, finishing Jasmin's thought.

"Yeah, that really doesn't sound like a good plan. Maybe I should come with you. I can just run back and grab a couple of shirts. Or we could just drive up there—" He started pulling the SUV off the road to swing back around.

"No!" said both Torie and Jasmin in unison.

The car lurched as Elric jerked the wheel before steadying it back on the road.

"I mean, thank you," said Torie, "But we are going to be fine. We'll be gone for a day. Two at the most. Plus, you're really needed here. Something just feels off lately. I'd feel better knowing you're here watching Max's back."

"Plus, don't forget Leo," said Jasmin, giving Torie a quick glance.

"That's right," Torie said. "Who would look after him? You were looking forward to having some alone time with him, remember? I left his feeding schedule on the refrigerator door. No in between meal snacking, okay?"

Elric was focused on the road ahead, his brow furrowed. He must have sensed her staring at him because he gave her a quick glance and a smile. "What? Oh, yeah right. No, don't worry. The little guy's in good hands."

Torie frowned but went back to watching the foliage race by. In no time, Elric was easing the car to a stop in front of the North-Northwest airline terminal. Outside, they hurried to the back and started hauling out their bags. The noise of departing jets, blaring horns and loud voices put Torie a bit on edge, but she took the time to wrap her arms around Elric and promised to call him as soon as they landed. He gave her a quick kiss, and nervously shook hands with Jasmin, before pulling her in for a hug.

"Please take care of her," he whispered into her ear.

She gave him a reassuring squeeze on the shoulder, and they parted. Torie looked over her shoulder and waved as they pushed their way through the revolving door and into the crowded airport. Taking one look at the long check-in line and the even longer security line, she groaned.

"And now the fun part," she said to Jasmin.

Forty-five minutes later, they were sitting at their gate, waiting for boarding to start. Torie sipped on a water and Jasmin snacked on a bag of chips they had picked up at one of the seemingly endless shops lining the halls to all gates.

"I can't believe they have the nerve to charge these prices," Jasmin said. "This bag was more air than chips."

"We should have just tried a teleportation spell to get there," said Torie.

"I told you about that. It's one thing when we did it around here, moving from one place to another around Singing Falls. But over such a great distance? With no ley lines to guide us and make paths? It would have been too dangerous. We could have gotten lost and ended up who knows where."

Torie sighed, sitting back against hard plastic. "I know.

You're right. I just hate being away, even for just a couple of days. Don't you think people have been acting weird? I mean, what was up with that shifter on Main Street? I've never seen one act like that."

Jasmin didn't speak but slowed down on the chips as she stared at the crowd passing by. "I don't know," she finally said, "But you're right. Something has felt off for a while now. But I can't put my finger on it."

"Can we fly?" Torie asked, leaning in close to whisper in her friend's ear.

Jasmin looked around, confused. "Um, yeah. That's what we're doing here. At the airport. Girl, please don't tell me you're about to start acting all loopy too..."

Torie frowned. "What? No, don't be ridiculous. I mean literally. Like in the movies. Maybe with a broom."

Jasmin leaned away from her, opening her eyes wide. "Have you bumped your head? I'll tell you what. I knew a forest witch once who was convinced with the right combination of plants and herbs she could do that. Had a special broom that she talked to and everything. Climbed up on her roof, recited an ancient incantation she found and took off."

Torie's breath caught in her chest. "So, it can be done then?"

Jasmin frowned again. "No, girl, she fell off that roof and broke her back when she landed on a big old rock in front of her house."

Torie huffed. "You could have just said that from the beginning."

Jasmin gave her a slight chuckle. "I know how you are once you start to get an idea in your head. I wanted you to see the full picture."

They sat in silence until it was time to board. Once seated, Torie texted both Fionna and Elric to let them know the flight was underway. She closed her eyes and reached for the wards that protected her home once again.

Elric was more than capable of protecting himself and Leo, but she felt a small measure of relief in knowing there was an added layer of protection around those she loved.

"Ready for this?" Jasmin asked with a smile. "Next stop, the hallowed homeland of our kind."

Torie closed her eyes and inhaled deeply. As much as she wished otherwise, something told her this trip was going to open doors to some very dark places.

Chapter Four

The city of Salem greeted the two witches with a unique blend of sensations as only it could. The crisp and cool air brushed across their skin as the fragrance of burning firewood and freshly baked apple-cider donuts swirled around them. Faint whispers of the salty sea breeze intertwined with the aroma of fallen leaves created an alluring and invigorating atmosphere.

They had deliberately asked the driver to drop them off within walking distance of their bed and breakfast so they could get a feel for the historic city. Everywhere they looked, their eyes feasted on the vibrant colors on display before them. Rich shades of red, orange, and yellow from the changing leaves danced in the gentle breeze and created a mesmerizing tapestry against the clear blue sky.

The historic architecture, a mix of colonial and Victorian that was adorned with intricate wood carvings and elegant ironwork, showcased the city's deep-rooted history.

As they wandered down Chestnut Street, a variety of art installations and eclectic shops drew their attention, their windows enticed the witches with colorful displays and unique wares.

"This is beautiful," said Jasmin. "Downtown Singing Falls is really going to need to step it up."

They paused at a storefront window for a pastry shop, the delicate aromas of hot apple cider mixed with the scent of freshly baked pies called to them.

They looked at one another and shook their heads, laughing as they continued.

"I would gain way too much weight living in a city like this," said Torie.

Turning away from the historic district, they made their way down a tree lined street towards a Federal-style bed and breakfast. Two signs greeted them. One announced the name of the bed and breakfast as The Witch's Whisk, and a second that proclaimed the structure was on the city's list of official historic registry homes.

They made their way through the meticulously landscaped grounds that showcased a vibrant flower bed and neatly trimmed hedges. A gently curving brick pathway guided them to the welcoming front door. A pair of ornate brass door knockers and a polished brass kick plate accented the entrance, while a vintage lantern overhead cast a warm, golden glow on the doorstep.

The door creaked slightly and was accompanied by the gentle tinkle of a tiny bell to announce their arrival. The spacious foyer greeted them with warm colors, classic wallpaper patterns, and white wainscoting that had been meticulously maintained. Rich, honey-colored floors creaked softly beneath their feet as they made their way through the entrance.

To their right was a drawing room filled with antique furniture and dominated by a fireplace with a beautiful carved wooden mantel. To their left was another, smaller room, outfitted with two high-backed chairs sitting in front of a grand, intricately carved desk. Behind the desk a sign hung on the wall that stated, "Welcome One and All".

Behind the desk sat a middle-aged woman dressed in a black flowing gown, with rings adorning every finger. She wore large, bedazzled, horn-rimmed glasses with a silver chain attached to hold them around her neck once removed. She smiled warmly and bowed her head. Her name tag read Lilith in elaborate typography.

"Welcome and be well, sisters," she said, her voice filled with respect and awe. "I take it your travels were good to you?"

Torie and Jasmin exchanged glances before Torie gave her a polite nod. "Indeed, they were. Thank you for asking."

"They were a little stingy with the peanuts," said Jasmin, earning a tiny poke from Torie's elbow. "But otherwise, it was great."

Torie handed over a print-out of their reservation number and pre-approved check-in to the receptionist.

After looking over it, the woman smiled. "Everything is in order for your stay. You have the two nicest suites available, at the top of the stairs, to the right." She frowned slightly as she was looking at the computer screen where she seemed to be verifying everything. "How fortuitous for you. It seems the previous guests reserving those rooms both canceled at the same time. How odd."

Jasmin shrugged and gave Torie a surprised look. "How odd indeed."

Lilith finished checking them in, printed out a page from the computer and handed it to them along with two brass keys. "If you'd like, you can leave your bags here and I'll have them taken to your rooms. Also, we have complimentary tea, coffee and pastries each morning for you. And at dusk, feel free to join us for our nightly blessing and giving of thanks to the great mothers for whom all things are possible. It's a sacred ceremony for all witches and is held in our lovely gardens out back."

Jasmin and Torie exchanged glances.

"Oh, um, yes, that sounds lovely," said Torie. "And we will be fine with our own bags, but thank you." She turned to pick up her bag, but then remembered something. "Oh, Lilith, you wouldn't happen to have a map of the town, would you? Maybe one that also lists all the magic shops in the area as well as the sites?"

Lilith smiled and held up a hand. "I have just the thing." She reached into one of the desk drawers, rifled through some papers, then held up a folded map. "This has everything you will need." She dropped her voice to little more than a whisper. "Things you won't find on a website." She gave them a wink and handed it over.

"Thank you," Torie said as they turned to leave.

Lilith loudly cleared her throat to get their attention. "That will be seven dollars."

"Oh. Of course it will be," said Jasmin, fishing in her bag for the money.

They made their way up the stairs to two rooms separated by a shared bath. Each room was well appointed and comfortable with wallpaper consisting of beautiful flowers in a welcoming sage and cream color. The focal point of each room was a grand, four-poster queen-size bed, the intricately carved wooden frame was draped in crisp, white linens with an abundance of plush, velvety pillows. The rooms also boasted an upholstered armchair, nestled in the corner beneath a cozy reading lamp as well as a beautiful, antique wooden armoire, providing ample storage for belongings.

After unpacking, they had agreed to meet in the garden behind the house to discuss their next steps. The garden itself was easily the best feature of the bed and breakfast.

It was a harmonious blend of New England charm and whimsical enchantment that took the witches breath away. Cobblestone pathways, lined with fragrant lavender and rosemary, guided them through the landscape, where a diverse array of colorful blooms that were designed to change with the seasons, greeted them. There were a variety of cozy seating areas; each offered a unique vantage point from which to admire the surroundings. They chose an elegant wrought-iron bench, nestled beneath the dappled shade of a graceful weeping willow that happened to be far enough away from the main house that no one would overhear their conversation.

"You know," said Torie, as they took a seat, "for a place steeped in lore and magical history, I haven't felt the slightest bit of magic here since stepping foot off the plane."

"I was thinking the same thing. I've even sent out little beacon spells to see what residual energies we might be able to tap into. Nothing. It's like this is the magical equivalent of a dry county. Not a drop to be found anywhere."

"And don't even get me started on Lilith and her blessing ceremony, or whatever she called it. If she's a witch then I'm a lion shifter," added Torie.

She had the map of the area spread open between them on the iron bench. It had the streets broken down, as well as the outlying parks and shore attraction. Along the main streets there were stars at certain intervals to denote stops of great importance to any self-proclaimed witch.

"Do you think the iron in the chair will cause interference?" Torie asked. "Should we move over to one of the rocks, or maybe just place it directly on the ground?"

Jasmin shook her head. "No, I don't think it will matter. There doesn't seem to be any ambient mystical energy in the air to begin with, so if anything, the iron might amplify our signal."

With that, she reached into her purse and took out an oblong-shaped gem that dangled from the end of a silver chain. The gem was a cross between white and pink and came to a point at the end that wasn't connected to the chain.

She held one end of the chain so that the gem hung freely over the map. Then, closing her eyes, she began to recite a spell.

"Whispers hidden, shadows flee,
reveal what's veiled, now come to me.
In this chant, I call forth sight,
to pierce the veil and bring to light,
the one concealed by forces strong or weak,
by the power of the Hex, gift me the one I seek."

At first nothing happened. The crystal hung suspended in space, determined to crush the witches' hopes of an easy solution to their problem. But then slowly, the gem responded to the incantation by pulling against her hand, straining to make contact with the map. Jasmin looked up at Torie and smiled before releasing the chain. The gem flew downward, stabbing into the map and standing straight, before then falling to the side, its job complete.

Jasmin picked up the gem and returned it to her bag. "Well, that was easier than I thought it would be. Looks like our friend Rowena possesses a pretty big magical signature."

She picked up the map, staring at the pinpoint hole the gem had created. "And she's not too far away."

Torie took a deep breath and released it slowly. "Are you ready? I don't see any point in putting this off any longer."

"Agreed. It looks like this place is just outside of town limits. There's nothing on the map around it. Looks like an area on the bluffs."

They made their way back inside the house and to their rooms. Even though the weather was nice, the New England air was crisp and promised to be even chillier by the ocean. Light jackets were the order of the day, as well as comfortable footwear.

Once they had everything needed for their excursion, Torie used her phone to call a rideshare for them. They climbed into the back of the black sedan and watched as the driver pulled up the address on the car's navigation system. He looked at the address, then over his shoulder and finally back to the address again.

"You want to go here?" he said, pointing to the map destination.

"Yes. Is there a problem?" asked Jasmin.

He hesitated before slowly shaking his head. "No. There is no problem. It's just that, this isn't a place for tourists. There is nothing for you to see here. If you want, I can suggest much better places where you can enjoy the ocean views."

The witches looked at one another briefly before Torie offered the driver a smile. "No, that's okay. We want to go there, please."

Finally, the driver shrugged his shoulder and turned his attention to the road as they pulled away from the bed and breakfast. They made the trip in silence, the only sounds in the car came from the radio as Garth Brooks tried to encourage them not to break his heart.

Twenty minutes later, the car came to a stop. Looking out the window Torie and Jasmin saw nothing to mark where they were. At some point, they had pulled onto a two-lane road barely wide enough for two cars to pass. The remoteness of the road was surprising considering how close it was to a major tourist attraction.

Torie leaned forward in her seat. "Is this it? I don't see anything."

The driver raised his shoulders. "You said you wanted to come here. Well, here we are." He half turned to face them. His eyes were hard as he stared at them. "What you are looking for is straight ahead. Just follow the path through the tall grasses. This is as far as I can take you."

"How do you know what we are looking for?" asked Jasmin, a hint of suspicion creeping into her voice.

The driver broke into a huge grin. "The bluffs, right? That's all you'll find there." He cocked his head to one side as they climbed out of the car. "Of course, if you do find something else...well, just remember, you sought it out."

Chapter Five

The path before them was sand, interspersed with gravel and larger rocks protruding upward, threatening a turned ankle if stepped on. Flanking the path were tall reeds and wild grasses that swayed gently in the breeze. The smell of salt was strong and pleasant, and the two women took in deep breaths, relishing the sea air.

"We don't get this up on our mountain," said Jasmin.

"I do love the ocean," said Torie. "Nothing quite like it."

"What do you think that driver meant by 'we asked to come here'? And was it just my imagination or was he trying to steer us clear of this area?"

"No, it definitely wasn't your imagination. I picked up on that too," Torie answered.

They trudged on for another five minutes before the path stopped, opening onto a dune of white sand and green grass that gradually sloped to a more dangerous incline. They made their way into the opening as far as they could, peering over the incline to see it fall precipitously to a rocky shore with the waves of the Atlantic Ocean crashing against cliffs far below.

"Whoa," said Torie, fighting off a wave of vertigo as she pulled back from the edge.

Jasmin looked around, only seeing more cliffs and jagged rocks in either direction. "Well, this can't be right."

"Are you sure the locator spell worked?" Torie asked.

"You saw it. By all accounts it was dead on. Rowena has to be here."

Torie looked back at the path from which they had come. "Maybe we missed something. A turn off or a split in the path. Let's double back and keep our eyes open."

Begrudgingly, they headed back for the path, but before entering it, something out of the corner of her eye caught Torie's attention. She stopped, looking to her left, staring at the wild grass there.

"What is it?" asked Jasmin, training her eye in the direction her friend was looking. "I don't see —" She stopped, narrowing her eyes.

"What is that?" questioned Torie.

Jasmin slowly shook her head. "Maybe it's a trick of the light…"

"No. It might be a trick, but it's not coming from the light." She drew on her magic, focusing her vision to perceive what was almost invisible to the naked eye.

There was a distortion there. Subtle, barely noticeable. Had they not been moving, she might not have caught it at all. No, it wasn't just that they were moving, it was that *it* was moving with them. And now that they stopped, it had stopped as well.

Jasmin had her hand behind her, and Torie could feel the magic she was summoning.

"Careful," Torie whispered. "We don't want to spook it."

"Yeah. It's the one that's scared right now," Jasmin replied. "What do we do?"

"Hold on. Let's try tact with whatever it is." She cleared her throat and spoke up, loudly. "I'm not stupid. I know a glamour when I see one. You might as well come on out."

The reeds rustled as the wind picked up, whipping about the two witches.

"Who are you?" came a voice, floating to them on the wind.

"My name is Torie, and this is my friend Jasmin. We have come seeking someone."

"And who is it that you seek?" came the voice.

"A woman known as Rowena," said Jasmin, fighting to keep her voice strong.

The wind was silent, dying down to little more than a gentle breeze. "Then you have come here for nothing. There is no one here by that name."

Torie sensed that whatever presence they were speaking with was starting to fade, a mystical ephemera that was retreating to wherever it had originated. Sensing that their only hope for finding a lead might be literally fading away, Torie acted.

She threw out her hand, sending her magic in the direction of the apparition. Her power became an extension of her physical self and allowed her to grab at the distortion before it could fully disappear. Though she couldn't see it, she could most definitely feel it.

It felt like she had grabbed the proverbial tiger by the tail.

She grunted, feeling herself pulled forward by the

strength of whatever she had made contact with. She turned her head to Jasmin. "Help me!"

Jasmin drew on her own magic and sent it flaring outward, encircling the same entity Torie had grabbed. Together, the witches wove a restraint, sensing that they would not be able to keep it in place for long against what felt like a force of nature.

"You dare," came the wind again. There was no anger in the voice. If anything, the witches sensed amusement cast in their direction.

"I'm sorry about this," said Torie, gritting her teeth. "We just need information. I promise you, if it weren't a matter of life or death, we would never do something like this."

"Oh, well, as long as you promise," came the reply. This time, it was practically laughing at them.

"We just need an audience with Rowena," said Jasmin. "Can you at least tell us where to find her? Just do that, and we'll let you go."

This time the wind actually laughed at them. "*You?* Will let *me* go?" The wind picked up again, this time it scoured their skin with bits of sand. "You witches and your presumptions."

Now the wind picked up intensity, concentrating on the witches, forming a mini cyclone around them. They felt their magic getting swept up in the pull of the wind. The power they had sent out was being spun back against them, wrapping them in a cocoon of their own making. It felt like they were the stick surrounded by threads of cotton candy holding them firmly in place.

"What in the —" started Jasmin. "How is this possible?"

Torie's eyes were flaring orange as she tried in vain to recall her magic, keep it from working against them. But it was to no avail. Whatever was holding them seemed to have better control over her power than she did in the moment.

"What do we do?" she whispered to Jasmin.

"What *can* we do?" came her friend's reply.

"What indeed?" said the wind. This time it seemed closer, almost whispering in their ears.

"We only want to talk," said Torie, struggling against her own magic. "Don't make us fight."

Again, the laughter. "As if you could." It was more a statement of fact than a boast. "Tell me, witches, what would you do if I sent you over the cliff to crash into the water below?"

As if to emphasize the point, they felt themselves lifted off the ground. Torie panicked as helplessness washed over her. The question that ran through her mind wasn't *could* this creature do what she threatened but *would* she.

Just as the wind began to move them in the direction of the bluffs, she felt the touch of Jasmin's magic reaching out for her.

"We are most definitely not going out like that," said Jasmin.

As they had done so many times in the past, they synced their magic. Two minds became one, and together, they called to their power.

> *"We call upon the powers of our ancestors past,*
> *to grant us strength and make our magic last.*
> *Our will is strong, our spirit true,*
> *And with this spell, we break free anew."*

Immediately, their power flared, responding to their call. Ethereal light swirled around them forming a chain that stabbed into the ground beneath them, anchoring them in place against the howling wind. Slowly, they used their power to pull them back down until their feet were once again on terra firma.

Feeling themselves anchored in place renewed their belief in their own magic. Eyes glowing, they turned their attention to the formless figure toying with them. They felt the wind rage in response, but now that they had a grip on their power, they refused to be moved. Together, they began to chant once more.

"Unseen foe, who seeks to hide,
but with this spell, your cloak subsides.
I summon the power of sight and sound,
and bring your form to the earthly ground."

The earth groaned and air around them boiled in response, but the witches held fast to their resolve. Magic chewed at the air around them, coloring the space with vapors of power that snaked around their unseen foe, forcing them into the light.

In an instant they were staring at the form of a woman who appeared to be middle-aged. She was tall and lithe of build. Her silver hair was pulled back from her face in a ponytail, highlighting high cheekbones and golden-hued eyes that reminded Torie of a lion. They didn't need to call her by name. Her resemblance to the woman in the picture Max had found was unmistakable.

"You," Torie hissed.

Rowena looked down at her hands in disbelief before addressing the women. "In the flesh it would seem."

Together, Torie and Jasmin focused on maintaining control of their magic as they faced the woman.

"Nice trick," said Rowena. "I had always heard the

power of the hex was almost incalculable. I admit I never really believed it. But you can't argue with what your own eyes are telling you." Again, she stared incredulously at her now visible form.

"We bind you in place," said Jasmin, making a fist so that their power tightened on the woman. "Let's see how you like it."

"Oh, please," said Rowena. She waved her hand nonchalantly, and the power that held her melted away in a shimmer. "I admit, you caught me by surprise. But don't make the mistake of thinking you and I are playing on the same field." Golden eyes flashed at the women as Rowena narrowed her gaze.

"How did you do that?" said Torie. "And how do you know we are hex witches?"

Rowena shrugged, smiling. "Only the power of the hex could bring me forth in mortal form. And I can smell it on you. As for how I broke your enchantment…that's simple. Your magic is powered by your intent and will. My will is greater than yours."

"What are you?" demanded Torie.

Her smile widened. "This is neither the time nor the place to get into something like that."

"Doesn't look like we're going anyplace anytime soon," said Jasmin. "So why don't you indulge us?"

The witches took a step back as Rowena slowly stepped forward. "I believe you said you were looking for me. Is that the question you mean to ask me? Because I may not feel like answering a second one. So, is that really what you want to know?"

Jasmin opened her mouth to speak, but Torie interrupted her. "No, that isn't what we want to know. Are you familiar with something called the Umbrali?"

Rowena's head lifted slowly, and her golden eyes focused so intently on Torie that the witch feared she might burn under the heat of their glare.

"Where did you hear that word?" asked Rowena.

"It was the dying words of someone we were trying to help," said Torie. "We think it's a cabal of some kind, but we don't know for sure."

"And what make you seek me out?" asked Rowena.

"We were able to track you here after finding a picture of you with the person we were trying to help," said Jasmin.

During the conversation, Rowena had continued to walk slowly towards them. As she approached, she had been waving one hand at her side. Rotating her wrist, her fingers flowing in the air as she spoke. The movement was so subtle the witches didn't know what was happening until the magic she wove reared itself before them.

"What are you doing?" asked Torie, sensing a threat. She reached for her own magic, only to find it once again not responding to her.

Vertigo again swept over the witches as the air around them bent and blurred. Their vision was clouded by fog, and both women found themselves pinching their eyes shut and shaking their heads to try and refocus. There was a moment of disorientation and sinking. For a split-second Torie feared Rowena had made good on her promise to fling them over the cliff.

But when they opened their eyes, the sandy area around them was gone.

They were no longer outside. Thatched walls with long, trailing vines hanging from the mud ceiling above them dangled everywhere. The space smelled of freshly dug earth, with the only source of illumination being a large candle sitting in the middle of the ground before them that burned without giving off heat.

Torie and Jasmin reached for one another, fighting the waves of nausea that threatened to overtake them.

"What...where are we?" asked Torie.

Rowena stepped forward, standing between them and the candle. "You're inside the mountain. And now I'm going to ask you some questions. And if you hesitate, or lie to me, I'll leave, and this will be your tomb."

Chapter Six

The air inside the space was stifling. How was it possible to be suffocating and cold at the same time? Jasmin held out her hand, summoning light, only to have it flicker and die in the palm of her hand.

"This is my domain," said Rowena. "Your magic, powerful as it is, won't help you here."

Torie took slow deep breaths, trying to steady herself as a memory closed in on her. Her nightmare came roaring back to her in vivid detail. Only now she realized it was more than just a dream. It was a vision that was now coming true.

The earth had opened and swallowed her whole. Just like it had every time she closed her eyes for the past week.

"You," she breathed, as she stared at Rowena. "You've been in my dreams. You are what has been haunting me."

Rowena frowned. "I can assure you I have done no such thing. I have never laid eyes on you before you came unbidden into my lands."

Torie ignored her, turning her head to Jasmin. "This is

it. This is what I've been experiencing lately. The feel of the earth pulling at me, sucking me down into blackness. This is where I end up. I know it is."

"Just breathe. We're getting out of here," replied Jasmin.

"Yes, you will," said Rowena. "As long as you answer me truthfully."

"What do you want to know?" demanded Torie. Her voice was ragged, and her breathing labored.

"Tell me the name of the person who told you about the Umbrali," she said.

"Eliza," Torie answered without hesitation. "Her name was Eliza. She led a coven of hedge witches."

Rowena didn't answer, but her eyes suddenly burned brighter than the candle. "And you said that she…passed. What do you mean by that?"

"We mean that she died," said Jasmin. "And her last words were a warning to us to beware the Umbrali."

The flame on the candle behind Rowena erupted, leaping high enough into the air to singe the vines on the ceiling.

"Do not lie to me!" Rowena screamed. "I told you what would happen if you did. I will seal you inside this mountain for all eternity, witches."

"Why would we make something like that up?" breathed Torie.

The candle flame, and the heat from Rowena's eyes lowered in intensity. "Because I would have known if that happened. I would have felt it. How exactly did she die?"

Torie and Jasmin exchanged glances, hesitating just long enough to draw Rowena's ire again.

"You? What did the two of you do?" Rowena said, the air around her crackling.

Torie swallowed hard. "Her body was destroyed, burned

to cinder. But she saved herself by jumping into the body of her sentinel protector. Only, she was losing herself inside that body. She couldn't maintain who she was and was slipping away. And she didn't want the body of the sentinel to fall into the wrong hands, so…" She didn't need to finish the sentence.

"You destroyed the body," said Rowena, softly.

"She was in pain," said Jasmin.

"Yes. For one such as her to lose themself…it would be like a tiny death lived over and over again. It was a kindness you did her," Rowena answered.

The oppressive atmosphere surrounding them lifted. The witches couldn't quite put their finger on what changed, but even though they were still confined within the same dungeon-like room, the tightness began to dissipate. The dark lightened, and it felt like the walls and ceiling retreated, opening, allowing them to breathe easier.

Torie stood up, taking in deep breaths as she looked around. How was Rowena doing this? She could tell from the look on Jasmin's face that she was wondering the same thing.

"I'm sorry for your loss," said Jasmin. "She obviously meant something to you."

Rowena sighed. "She was my Gorlaith."

The witches waited for her to continue, and when she didn't, Torie spoke up. "What is a Gorlaith?"

"In my original tongue, it roughly means blue princess. It is the designation given to the leader of my followers. Namely, those whom you have named hedge witches."

Jasmin cleared her throat. "And what does that make you?" Rowena cast a hard look in her direction. "Come on. We already know you're at least two hundred years old. Are you a vampire?"

Rowena's eyes widened. "How dare you? I would never associate with such low born creatures. I am a Cailleach. I am the earth mother from which the hedge witches draw their power."

Jasmin's eyes grew even larger. "Are you telling us you're an earth goddess?"

This brought a smile to Rowena. "Some have referred to me as that. But I am not divinity. At least not in the definition of your modern language. But I have been around for a very long time, lending my power to my followers."

Torie stared at the woman, not sure how to even address the questions that were forming in her mind. "Have you always lived here? In Salem, I mean."

"No. I was called here at a time of great upheaval in your world. My followers were being rounded up by men and killed. By the time I realized what was happening, it was too late. Many of my hedge witches, along with those who had nothing to do with the practice, had been hanged. Or crushed. My vengeance on those responsible was swift and merciless. And once that was done, I stayed here, rebuilding my followers and making sure the horrors that passed would never happen again."

"The witch trials," Torie whispered. "I can't imagine seeing our sisters burn."

"No. That was a misconception," said Rowena. "These men were cruel, but also very fearful. They feared that burning the women would give them time to utter a curse against their oppressors. So, the preferred method of killing witches during that time was to hang them or press them to death between large rocks. Either way, it rendered the witch breathless, so no spells or incantations could be uttered." Her gold eyes grew dark with memory. "Now, there *were* fires. That was how I dealt with those killers."

Jasmin was shaking. "The thought of what those poor women went through. And for what? Fear of something man didn't understand."

Rowena spat onto the dirt floor. "It wasn't fear. It was a chance for men to assert dominance in a way that had been denied to them in the country they immigrated from. They were a wicked lot, and here, on new shores, far from any eyes that could have condemned their behavior, they enacted rules based on subjugation and cruelty."

"Rowena, what made you stay? Even after your work was done?" Torie asked.

"Because if any place needed the protection of my witches, this new land was it. With the fear created in these women, I saw a chance to create something new. So, I created the first all-female coven. I bound this land so that its secrets were only available to women. That way, they would never have to know fear at the fists of men again." She looked at the witches, her eyes twinkling. "Much like your own power, hedge-craft was not meant to be wielded by men."

Torie frowned. "So, what happened?"

Rowena sighed. "Men covet what they think someone else has. So, they found a way to ingratiate themselves into the world of the hedges. But the power they were able to wield was limited. When they realized they could not draw power directly from me, they figured out a way to draw from the female witches around them."

Jasmin's eyes grew large. "That was how warlocks and sorcery started."

Rowena nodded. "Yes. Male witches who could steal the power of women around them."

"But we have seen male hedge witches who are part of

covens," said Torie. "They seemed to be welcomed into the coven."

"That is true," said Rowena. "I could not stop the slow infiltration without cutting my sisters off completely as well. Plus, eventually, my own presence was not needed for the covens. Their power was their own, to do with as they saw fit. They were self-governing, and if part of that governing meant letting men join their ranks, and eventually teaching them ways to tap into my gifts directly…well, I was not about to interfere." She gave the witches a look. "Besides, as you know, the men in my craft are not able to manipulate actual ley line magic. Unlike those in your covens."

Torie felt as if someone had physically knocked the wind from her. She stared at Jasmin, whose eyes were wide.

"What are you talking about?" asked Jasmin. "There are no male hex witches. It's a birthright that is denied to them."

Rowena frowned at the women. "What are *you* talking about?"

"Hex magic is granted to women. Passed down from one generation to the next, presenting on a woman's fortieth birthday."

"There are no male hex witches," said Jasmin.

Rowena shook her head. "You poor children. This is what happens when we elders abandon our flocks. Our teachings are lost and eventually forgotten."

A chill started at the base of Torie's neck and quickly spread down her spine. Her throat was thick, and it felt like she had swallowed sand.

"In hedge-craft, the men are weaker because they were never granted the ability to tap the source of hedge witch power directly. But with your kind, the men were the first to master the power of the hex. It was they who used that power to bind the power of female hex witches until their fortieth birthday." Her eyes flared golden once again. "In the world of hex magic, you are the rarity."

Neither Torie nor Jasmin could speak. Numbness spread across the witches as their minds spun, trying to comprehend the incomprehensible.

Rowena tilted her head to one side. "I thought you knew."

"No. We didn't," said Jasmin. "How would we?"

Rowena paused before continuing. "Because you asked about the Umbrali."

Torie looked at her, confused. "I don't see the connection."

"The Umbrali are an exceptionally powerful coven of male hex witches. And if they have their sights set on you or your town, then you are as good as dead."

Chapter Seven

"This needs to be an all-hands-on-deck assembly," said Jasmin. She and Torie were sitting in her great room, a bottle of cabernet and two filled glasses sitting before them.

"And tell them what?" asked Torie. "That an earth goddess told us that everything we thought we knew about our birthright has been a lie?"

"Or, and I'm just spit balling here, we tell them the cabal out to take over Singing Falls is made up of male hex witches who are probably capable of killing us all."

Torie looked at her friend, arching a single eyebrow. "That will just start a panic."

"Maybe they *should* panic," Jasmin answered. "And from the sound of things, it will take all of us to take on the Umbrali."

"Or we look into this cabal ourselves. Figure out what we're up against before we involve the others. I mean, if they are as dangerous as Rowena suggested, then do we want to risk bringing our friends into this conflict?"

Jasmin didn't answer as she studied her friend's face. Torie sighed, finally meeting Jasmin's eyes.

"I know you're right. I know that deep down. We stand a better chance of taking these monsters on working together. But if something happens to one of them…"

Jasmin reached for her friend and gave her hand a squeeze. "And if we go in alone, and they take us out, what do you think happens next?"

Torie nodded. "I know. You're right. As usual. I just wish we could have convinced Rowena to join us. Something tells me we could use the extra firepower."

Jasmin huffed. "Please. Who needs an earth goddess when you've got me?"

Torie's laughter nearly choked her it came out so quickly. She was thankful that as dire as things appeared, her friend was able to make her laugh out loud.

"Why do you think she refused to get involved?"

"You heard her," answered Jasmin, "this isn't her fight."

"Yeah, I don't buy that. There must be more to it than that. I'm pretty sure the cabal killed Eliza and the rest of the hedge witch coven. If she is their patron, that makes it her fight too. No. She's up to something."

"Maybe if we're lucky, she'll take them out for us."

"We need to find out more," Torie said. "More about Rowena and most importantly, more about the Umbrali."

"Have you come across anything in your mother's archives about male hex witches?" Jasmin asked.

Torie had recently cast a spell that let her absorb much of her mother's written tomes and grimoires. What she hadn't been able to absorb magically she had spent hours manually going over. "No. There has never been a hint of anything like that."

"We knew about male warlocks," Jasmin said. "But a full-blooded male hex witch? I would have never thought something like that was even remotely possible."

"That means she wasn't told about them," Jasmin added. "Your mother was an incredible witch. And very thorough. If she had an inkling there was a threat out there like this, she would have let me know."

Torie felt a stab of sadness at Jasmin's words. She wasn't jealous of her friend's relationship with her mother, but there were times when she not only missed having her mother around, but also mourned the time lost that she could have spent learning from her.

She sat back with a sigh. "I just don't know where to start looking for answers."

"Well, typically, the best place to start is at the beginning," said Jasmin. "Where all this started. The hedge witch mansion."

"Max and Elric already swept that place," Torie said. "There was no trace of who – or what – killed the coven."

"No offense to the wolves, they're certainly the best there is at tracking, but they aren't witches. If this cabal is made up of male hex witches –"

"Then they might have left signatures the wolves wouldn't be able to pick up," Torie completed.

"But we could."

"Yes!" Torie said, unable to contain the excitement sweeping through her.

"When do we leave?"

Torie looked at her watch. "I need to get back to the house for dinner. Elric will be wondering what we're up to."

They had decided to meet and unpack everything they learned in Salem at Jasmin's house. As good as Elric's ears were, she was pretty sure he wouldn't be able to hear them from one house to the other. Between him and Leo, they thought speaking freely at Jasmin's was preferable to having to explain something before they were ready.

"Do you want to join us?" Torie asked. "It's turkey lasagna night."

Jasmin pursed her lips. "I do love a good turkey lasagna. But no. I've got some things I want to look into here. Besides, we just got back from Salem. You need some time alone with your man. And that little dragon of yours. You know how he gets when he hasn't seen you in a while. I do not have the strength to fight him off right now."

Torie smiled. "Tell you what, why don't you come over for breakfast in the morning? I'll invite Max and Fionna as well. She can get those kids she hired to open for her. They'll be fine for a couple of hours. That way, we can talk to everyone at once."

Jasmin smiled. "Everything is going to be fine. I can feel it."

Torie let out a nervous breath as she got up to leave. She had a feeling as well, but it wasn't quite as optimistic as that of her friend.

They said their goodbyes, and Torie found herself lost in her own thoughts as she made the walk from Jasmin's house to her own. The woods were quiet, unlike her own thoughts, which seemed to be firing a mile-a-minute.

Something wasn't adding up. If Rowena was who she claimed to be, and Torie had no reason to believe otherwise, why wasn't she adding her strength to theirs? Why wasn't she here with them now, helping to right a horrible wrong?

No matter how much she claimed to be above the affairs of humans, Rowena had her own agenda. Torie was sure of it. She had seen the way the goddess had reacted when she found out about the death of Eliza and her coven.

Goddess.

Torie shook her head in dismay. She thought back to her life of leisure and luxury that she had lived five short years ago. Any and everything she wanted had been at her disposal. If she didn't already have it, acquiring it was just a short, quick swipe of a black American Express card away. Back then, she realized nothing had value because she never thought anything about all the stuff she hoarded; there was no personal attachment to it. Other than the gifts from her son, nothing really stuck with her.

It was all just *stuff*.

She valued the people in her life. She knew that she was incredibly lucky to have all that she did, but still, it took the tragedy of a divorce, a public scandal, and losing everything for her to realize what was really important and lasting. But even then, when she first moved to Singing Falls and discovered she was a descendant of a long line of powerful witches, she would never have been able to imagine that she would one day come face to face with a living goddess.

But life had a way of working out for the best. The life she had created in Singing Falls, the friends she had made, the experiences she'd had. All of it had combined to make something truly magical. In every sense of the word. In many ways, this was the first time she had felt alive. Everything she had known before Singing Falls was from a different life. One that consisted of hazy, dream-like memories that seemed to belong to someone else.

This was her place now. Her rock. And she would fight any demon from hell or monster from another realm to protect it.

She heard the sound of breaking glass and crashing furniture, followed by Elric's roar just as she caught sight of her house. Breaking into a run, she hit the door with her magic, casting it open as she rushed through, drawn to the sounds of a struggle coming from the large, open sitting area off the main entrance. She burst into the room, hands glowing with power, and stopped short, not sure what to make of what was going on.

In front of her was a broken coffee table and couch cushions that had been shredded and thrown onto the floor. In the middle of the ruined furniture was Elric in full wolf form, rolling around on the ground with Leo clutched in his massive paws. The dragon was huffing excitedly, trying to dislodge Elric's mouth from around his neck.

Torie screamed. "Elric! What are you doing? Get off him!"

Immediately both of them looked up, eyes like deer caught in headlights. Elric shifted back to human and untangled himself from the little dragon. Leo dropped to the floor and began licking at the scales running along his back with a reptilian tongue.

"Oh, sorry about that," said Elric, rushing over to Torie. He was jumping up and down in place as he smiled at her. "We were just playing and got carried away."

Torie's eyes traveled over the destruction around the room. "Playing? You broke half the furniture in here."

Elric looked around, a shocked expression on his face. He took a deep breath, running his fingers through his hair. "Wow. I guess I didn't realize. Hey, but don't worry, I can fix this." He turned to wade into the mess, and Torie reached out a hand, beckoning to him.

"No, It's okay. We can clean this up later. Why don't you go get cleaned up and take Leo with you? I'll start dinner and then we can tackle this…tomorrow maybe?"

Elric spun around dramatically, giving her a playful salute before motioning for Leo to follow him as he rushed out of the room heading for the stairs.

"And no rough housing in the bedroom!" Torie called after them, before again turning to survey the mess. She sighed as a broom, dustpan and mop appeared in the doorway and began cleaning. She shook her head, muttering. "Oh, now you show up."

She made her way to the kitchen and removed a Tupperware container with premade red sauce from the freezer. She opened the refrigerator door to get some ground turkey meat and gasped. The inside of the refrigerator was a mess with open and spilled containers of food. There were pieces of chicken and bacon strewn along the shelves and splashes of milk everywhere. Slamming the door, she snatched out her cell phone and hastily dialed Jasmin.

"I was just about to call you," said Jasmin, a little out of breath.

"What's going on?" asked Torie, concern rising in her voice.

"I just got a distress call from Glen. She's worried about Fionna."

Torie frowned. "Let me guess. There's something off about her behavior."

"Well, if you consider refusing to quit eating as strange behavior, then yes. Apparently, they are at the bakery and… well, she says we have to see for ourselves."

"Be out front in five minutes. I'll swing by and pick you up."

She hung up and cast a glance upwards at the ceiling. Making her way to the bottom of the stairs, she called out.

"Elric, I need to run to the bakery for a bit. Are you going to be okay?"

He called back to her in a singsong voice. "I'll be fine. Just going to grab some SunChips and watch some television, I think. And don't worry, I'll take good care of Leo."

"Yeah, that's what I'm worried about," Torie whispered to herself as she grabbed her keys and made her way out of the house.

Chapter Eight

"Why didn't you seem surprised at what I told you about Fionna?" Jasmin asked.

They were in the car and had just pulled into a parking spot in front of the bakery. Walking towards the entrance, Torie looked over at her friend. "Because something weird is happening with Elric as well. I think something is going on with the shifters in town."

Jasmin stopped, staring at her friend. "Based on two of them acting strange? And what do you mean by weird when it comes to Elric?"

"Not just two of them. Remember that shifter who bumped into us on the sidewalk? And his reaction? I'd never seen anything like that before. And as for Elric, well, he was rolling around on the floor in wolf form, wrestling with Leo. And he was in a very playful and joking mood."

Jasmin's eyes grew wide. "Elric was joking? And playing?" She shook her head. "Yeah. Something's not right."

Together they walked into the bakery to find it empty.

Nicholas, one of Fionna's newest hires, came rushing from the back of the bakery, pointing to the kitchen.

"They're in the back," he said, his voice rushed and strained. He was wringing his hands together, his eyes wide and searching. "We called Glen, and when she couldn't figure out what to do, she called you guys."

"Hey, whatever it is, it's okay," said Jasmin, trying to calm the young man. "What's going on?"

He was shaking his head. "I have no idea. Fionna was acting a little off all day, but then…I mean, she was so hungry, and now…there's something wrong with her face… me and Tara had no clue what to do." His eyes stared into the distance. "I've never seen someone look like that before."

Torie and Jasmin exchanged looks before heading through the swinging doors to the industrial kitchen.

"Um, maybe you should hang back here," Jasmin suggested, turning to Nicholas as he attempted to follow them. "Just in case someone comes in, I mean. And you look like you need to sit down for a bit."

Nicholas sank into a chair, eyes still distant. "Yeah. You're right about that…"

As soon as they entered the kitchen, Glen gave them a quick, hard stare. She was standing beside a seated Fionna, with Tara standing a bit farther back from them. The young employee had both hands to her mouth, her eyes wide in shock.

"I was just explaining to Tara that Fionna is having an allergic reaction to something she has eaten," said Glen, pointedly. "That everything is okay, it's just a reaction."

Fionna was sitting with her back to Jasmin and Torie, and as the two witches made their way around to face her, it took all their strength to suppress a gasp.

Fionna's face had elongated and narrowed. Her nose had become more button like, and quivered slightly as she looked around from eyes that had receded and become like two rare, black, polished bits of opal. Pronounced teeth and ears elongated into points completed the change in her features. She looked up at Torie and Jasmin in a silent plea.

"I've never seen a food allergy like that before," said Tara, taking a tentative step towards her boss.

"Oh no," said Jasmin, holding up a hand to stop her. "We've seen this before. And she gets very self-conscious around others when it happens. It's probably best if you stay over there. As a matter of fact, why don't you go out and keep Nicholas company while we…uh…"

"Give her the shot Glen asked us to pick up from the pharmacy," said Torie with a smile.

Tara frowned but began to slowly shuffle her way to the door. "Are you sure she's going to be okay?"

"She will be fine," Torie said. "But you look like you could use some water. It can be scary seeing her…allergies…for the first time. But she'll be back to her normal self in no time."

Torie and Jasmin waited patiently for the doors to swing shut behind Tara before turning to Glen.

"What in the world?" asked Jasmin.

"I don't know. I got a weird, almost nonsensical text from her, and when I replied…no answer. I thought that wasn't like her and then, I got a call from Tara saying Fionna seemed to be sick or something. I came right over and found her like this," Glen said. "I'm sorry about the allergy fib, it was all I could think of on the spot to tell Tara and Nicholas."

"No, you did the right thing," said Jasmin. "How long has she been like this? Has she spoken?"

Glen shook her head. "Not a word. And I noticed she was shifting in and out of her squirrel form more and more the last couple of nights. She just said she had a lot of excess energy to burn and would go for runs in the woods."

Torie stared at her. "Elric said the same thing. Said it was because of the full moon approaching. But I've known him for a while now. Yeah, he is usually a little more energetic during the run up to the full moon, but nothing like he's been exhibiting lately. Anything else out of the ordinary?"

Glen thought for a moment. "Just the nonstop eating. And her thoughts seemed to be a little scattered. But she just chalked that up to working longer hours here at the bakery." Her voice trailed off as she bit at her fingernail, staring intently at the woman she loved.

Torie took her by the elbow, giving it a reassuring squeeze. "She's going to be fine. I promise you. We need to get her to Emil. See if there is anything medically that could be causing this."

Jasmin turned, putting her phone back in her purse. "Way ahead of you. He said bring her over immediately."

"But first...a little glamour," said Torie. She focused her magic and waved a hand over Fionna's face. As she did, a shimmer crossed the squirrel shifter's features, rearranging them into the familiar face they all knew. "This way, no one will say anything while we get her out of here."

"Fionna, honey, we are going to take you outside, put you in the car, and drive over to see Emil, okay?" said Jasmin. She kept her tone even and low, making certain her friend didn't misinterpret anything she said.

"I don't even know if she understands us," said Glen, batting her eyes rapidly.

Torie could tell the woman was fighting to hold back

tears and all she could do was offer more encouragement. "She can hear us. The Fionna we know is a fighter. She's in there."

Glen offered her hand, and Fionna reached for it, letting her wife assist her out of the chair. Jasmin led the way as they walked through the metal doors and out into the cafe space.

Tara and Nicholas were sitting at a small table next to the cash register and both jumped up and rushed forward at the sight of the ladies. Fionna let out a tiny, high-pitched squeak at the sight of them and darted back behind Glen.

"It's okay," Torie said to the two youths. "As you can see, the shot is already starting to work. She's just still reeling from the allergy. We are taking her to the doctor now, just to be safe. Can you two handle things here for a bit?"

They both nodded, taking a step back.

"Tell her not to worry about anything here," Tara called after them as they left the building. "Just focus on getting better."

They managed to get Fionna and Glen into the back of Torie's car without incident or running into anyone else on the sidewalks. Torie backed out before gunning the engine, getting them through town to the medical plaza just behind the community hospital where Emil was waiting by the entrance.

It took a bit more coaxing to get Fionna out of the car than it did to get her into it. She had grown more and more skittish about her surroundings as they made the drive. She clung to Glen's hand, her grip growing more and more white knuckled until Torie and Jasmin feared she might break her wife's knuckles if she squeezed much more.

With Glen constantly reassuring her that everything was going to be okay, they were able to get the squirrel shifter into one of Emil's medical bays and sitting on an exam table. He looked at her, frowning a bit.

"You can remove the glamour spell," he said. "There's no one in here but us."

Torie passed her hand across Fionna's face, recalling the spell she had cast over the shifter. The air around Fionna wavered and everyone was then staring into a mask of suffering and fear that had replaced their friend. Her eyes darted wildly about the room, and she looked like she was ready to bolt at any moment.

"Interesting," said Emil, scratching his chin. "I haven't seen anything like this before."

"We have," said Torie. "There was a man who bumped into us on the sidewalk outside the bakery earlier this week. He was a shifter of some sort and for a split-second, his face changed into something along the lines of what we're seeing here with Fionna."

"What kind of shifter was he?" Emil asked.

"No idea. But he looked kind of...rodent," said Jasmin. "That sounds really ugly to say."

"It's like she's stuck in between shifting into her squirrel form, somehow," said Torie. "Kind of like Elric's hybrid wolf form. Could that be it?" She looked up at Glen. "Has that happened before?"

"Never once," Glen said.

"No, hybrid shifting is something unique to wolf shifters," said Emil. "It is a holdover in their evolution from the time when they were the daylight guardians of the vampires." His tone was absentminded as he continued to study Fionna.

Torie and Jasmin exchanged curious glances.

"Whoa, you can't just drop something like that," said Jasmin. "What are you talking about? Daylight guardians?"

Emil looked up, his eyes moving from one to the other. "I assumed you knew. I mean, the town sheriff is a werewolf and you – " he gestured to Torie – "Are mated to one."

"Hey now," said Torie, "I don't think *mated* is the right word there."

"Excuse me," said Glen, clearing her throat, "but can we maybe get back to –" She nodded fiercely at Fionna.

"Oh, of course," said Torie. "What was I thinking? Emil, any ideas as to what could be causing this?"

"I need to take some blood and run a panel. I also want to run a few other tests. I'll know more after I do that. Now, you said you saw another shifter exhibiting strange behavior. Have you noticed it with any others?"

Torie looked at Jasmin then cleared her throat. "Elric hasn't been himself lately. He's definitely acting out of character."

Emil gave her a sharp, steely-eyed look. "Interesting." He moved over to a table next to the door and withdrew a small needle and a couple of plastic tubes with different colored caps. With a nod to Glen, he pulled a rolling stool up to Fionna, needle poised. Glen placed an arm around Fionna's shoulders and pulled the woman into her chest, placing a comforting hand on the side of her face as she calmly rocked her. Emil moved swiftly, with precision honed over years of practice; cleaning the skin, inserting the needle, and collecting the vials of blood before Fionna could become more distressed.

"I will need a few hours to run all the tests I'd like," Emil said. "But I would suggest that she remain here during that time. I need to observe her physical behavior and any further changes she may go through." He glanced at Glen. "Are you able to stay with her? You are having a positive influence on her right now, and I would like that to continue."

Glen nodded emphatically. "I'm not going anywhere." She took Fionna's hand and gave it a loving squeeze.

"What about us, doc?" Jasmin said. "What can we do?"

One of the sprite's eyebrows shot upward. "I should think that would be obvious. We are clearly dealing with an outbreak of...something, that tends to be impacting the shifter community. Isn't there a particular shifter you should be checking in on, given their status and abilities?"

Torie frowned, considering his words. Then it hit her, and she turned to Jasmin, eyes open wide.

"Max."

Chapter Nine

"He's not answering," said Jasmin, swiping to close the screen on her cell.

Torie gripped the steering wheel harder as she headed out of downtown, making their way to the more secluded outskirts where Max rented a cabin. "He's not answering and neither did Elric. That bothers me. Something is just not right. Hey, try the police station. See if either of them is there."

"Good idea." She opened her screen and made a quick call. "Hi, I'm a friend of Max's and I can't seem to reach him. Is he there? Can you tell him Jasmin is on the phone for him? It's urgent." She nodded along to whatever the other person was saying, her body suddenly stiffening. "What? You're sure? Can you tell me where? Okay, fine. I understand." Closing the call, she turned her attention to Torie. "Apparently, he's been called out on a case. Domestic disturbance that required his attention."

Torie frowned, a knot forming in the pit of her stomach. "Do you know where?"

Jasmin shook her head. "They wouldn't tell me that. But she said he got the call on his personal line and told his deputies there was no need for them to respond."

"That means it's supernatural in nature," said Torie.

"And if that's the case, we – or rather you – should be able to home in on it if it involves a shifter."

Torie pulled over, easing the big SUV to a stop. "I've never tried something like that."

"You can do it. Your ability to sense and hear the thoughts of shifters should be able to pick up on anything that is so out of the ordinary it would cause one to call the police."

Torie closed her eyes and focused, reaching out with her magic. Almost at once, she grimaced, her face twisting into a mask of pain.

"What is it?" asked Jasmin.

"Anger. Aggression. Confusion." Torie looked over at Jasmin. "And it's all coming from Max."

"Can you tell where he is?" Jasmin asked.

Torie nodded, shifting the car into gear and pulling out. "He's at Emberwood Hollow. I recognized the large rock that sits at the entrance to the community."

"Oh, this can't be good," said Jasmin, sitting back in her seat.

"Well, on the plus side, I've always wanted to see the Hollow," said Torie, speeding up.

She followed Main Street out of town, making a right on an unmarked road that wound tightly between tall pine trees. At some point the asphalt beneath them turned to gravel and eventually became dry dirt. The canopy above them began to grow together, creating a living tunnel through which they traveled.

Ahead of them was a large stone marker in the shape of

a crescent moon rising from the earth. The car came to a stop in front of the rock, and the two witches climbed out.

"Looks like we are here," Torie said. "Have you been here before?"

"Only once," said Jasmin. "Like all of Singing Falls it's open to everyone who knows about the community. But most have no reason to venture into this part of town."

Torie reached out with her magic. "There are no wards here."

Jasmin shook her head. "No. They aren't really needed. This is a shifter community. Some very powerful shifters make their home here. You'd have to be very brave or very stupid to come here and start some mess."

Torie looked around as they walked. Once past the stone monolith, a dirt path led them to an open field over-flowing with wildflowers and soft grasses that, under different circumstances, she might have plopped down on just to enjoy the natural beauty and solitude around her. Ahead of them, the forest grew denser, but she could make out quite a few breaks in the woods where paths zigzagged and crisscrossed through the landscape.

Crossing the meadow, they entered the wooded area, the collage of greenery around them varied from emerald to pale lime and yellow. The valley, or hollow, as it was called in that part of the mountains, was a natural formation carved between two mountains by a river that snaked its way from the high country, down to the low-lying hills below the town of Singing Falls.

The town was named for the falls that fell gently across crystal rocks, creating a tinkling sound that rang out like chimes at the base of the river. And while she had heard of the mighty shifters who had long ago settled in the Hollow, she had never visited them.

Once inside the forested area, she could feel eyes on her, but when she turned to face them, there was no trace of who or what might have been watching.

"Are we being watched?" she asked in a whisper, her voice tinged with trepidation.

"Probably," Jasmin answered. "And you don't have to whisper. Trust me, the shifters living in Emberwood Hollow can hear you no matter what."

Torie wasn't sure if that made her feel better or worse. "If there is a problem with the shifters, this is the last place Max should be. And us too, probably."

"We need to make sure Max is okay," Jasmin said. "And let him know what's been going on. I just can't imagine what kind of issue would draw him out here." She stopped in her tracks, her head snapping around in Torie's direction.

Torie frowned in concern. "What is it?"

"There aren't just shifters here. Some of them are married. To humans."

Hastily, they plowed across the trail, pushing aside branches and vines that seemed to be reaching for them, trying in vain to slow their progress.

"Just once, I'd like to be rushing towards a crystal blue ocean with only hot sand in the way," huffed Torie. "Why is it always trees and briars scratching at us?"

"Well, for one thing, we live in the woods on a mountain. Not at the beach."

They were quiet as they broke through the forest into a second clearing. One that was dotted with small, wooden houses that were arranged the outer perimeter. Some were cozy cottage types, with small gardens in front, others were little more than thatched structures with crude openings cut into the rooflines to regulate heat. All of them opened in the back to rocky shales along a rushing river with steep, rocky cliffs for borders.

Torie looked up at the majestic mountains that created the natural borders for Emberwood Hollow and marveled at their beauty. Her admiration was cut short by a commotion from one of the cottages in the shared open courtyard.

An enormous man, tall and broad with a mane of dark curly hair and a full beard that threatened to swallow his facial features, stumbled out. He was followed by a smaller, frail-looking woman who clutched one arm to her side as she called after him.

A second man exited the house behind her, his eyes glaring yellow as his voice rose in timber, yelling at the hairy man to stop and stay where he was.

It was Max. And something had made him furious.

In response to the sheriff's hard voice yelling at him, the hairy man turned and stomped at the ground as his body seemed to swell. In seconds, a grizzly the size of a small camper stood in the middle of the yard, unleashing a roar that rattled Torie's teeth.

Max raced forward, jabbing his finger in the bear's direction.

"Horst, I'm ordering you right now to shift back to human. You are not going to be running amok here, causing all kinds of problems, hurting defenseless women, and taking no accountability," he yelled.

Torie and Jasmin were closer now and could see the spittle flying from Max's mouth as he countered the bears roar with his own screams.

"At least he isn't shifting," said Jasmin. "Hey, Max, what in the world is going on?"

Looking around, the witches noticed an audience had formed as more and more people had left their homes to watch. Murmurs drifted from everywhere, and Torie couldn't tell which, if any, were pro-Max.

Max whirled to face the witches. "What are you two doing here? I've got this." His eyes narrowed as he returned his attention to the bear shifter.

The woman who had come out of the house with them was trying desperately to get Max's attention. "Please… Sheriff, it wasn't his fault. He hasn't been himself lately, and I only called you because I didn't want him to possibly hurt anyone else. He didn't even know what he was doing, he just pulled away from me…that was all. He never meant to hurt me."

Max was breathing hard, his attention fully focused on the shifter. The bear dropped to all fours and began pacing back and forth, swinging his head and huffing at the ground.

"Don't you show aggression to me, bear. You will do exactly as I say. And I'm telling you to shift," Max said.

The bear stopped moving and focused on Max. A deep growl emanated from his chest, bouncing off the sheriff.

"Fine," Max said, his own form beginning to stretch and shift.

"No, please. I called you to help defuse the situation," pleaded the woman, reaching for Max.

The wolf was in mid-shift and swept her back with a wave of his hand. Seeing the woman be touched by Max set the bear shifter off, and he exploded forward, powerful paws propelling forward in an explosion of fur, muscle, and fangs.

Max stood his ground, having stopped his shift in hybrid form, so that he could hit the bear with a powerful fist. With a howl, Max leapt at the shifter, throwing his arms around the bear's massive bulk. With a heave, he lifted the creature and threw it away from him and the woman.

The bear landed, skidding on its paws before rearing up on its hind legs, fangs dripping, and claws raised.

Max licked his lips at the display, showing his own claws as he prepared to charge the shifter. In a blur, he launched himself, claws extended, aiming for the bear's exposed throat.

Emerald light surged as Jasmin threw her power at the wolf, holding him back and stopping his attack. "Torie, deal with the bear."

Torie nodded and extended her own magic, wrapping it around the bear shifter. Her power surged into the creature, soothing it, finding the centers of his power and triggering his return to the form of a man. Immediately, the man known as Horst looked about, dazed and blinking rapidly.

"What happened?" he asked. "How did I get out here?"

The woman raced to his side, grabbing his massive arm in hers. "Horst? My husband. Are you alright?"

"Diedre?" His eyes drifted to his wife and slowly recognition, followed by regret and horror, crept into them. "Oh no. Are you okay? Did I hurt you?" He gently touched her, placing his hand on her arm.

"No, I am fine. Do you remember anything?"

He was shaking his head and about to respond when he noticed the werewolf raging at him and being held back by magic.

"Sheriff?" he asked. "What are you doing here?" He approached the wolf, only to jump back a couple of steps as Max roared in anger, swiping at Jasmin's magic with his claws.

"Max, that's enough," said Torie, stepping in front of the raging wolf. "This isn't like you. You need to calm down...right now, before you hurt someone. Or worse."

Her words seemed to penetrate the shifter's rage, and he

dropped back, a frown crossing his lupine features. Slowly, as his anger receded, he returned to his human form, the same look of confusion falling across his features as had graced the bears.

Jasmin eyed the big wolf, making sure he was truly in the right frame of mind, before she lowered her magic and released him. His eyes moved from the witch to the bear shifter and his wife, her eyes wide with fear.

"Jasmin...Torie. What just happened?"

Chapter Ten

Max and the bear shifter sat together on a large log in the courtyard, each drinking massive amounts of water from large tumblers.

"You don't remember anything?" asked Jasmin.

Max shook his head between gulps. "No. I remember being in the office, getting the call that there was a potential domestic disturbance in the Hollows. Being that it was Emberwood Hollows, I figured I should take the call. I remember coming out here, making my way to the village and entering Diedre's house…and then it gets kind of fuzzy." He frowned, before shaking his head. "Next thing I know I'm standing there looking at you and Torie."

Jasmin glanced at Horst. "Same for you?"

The shifter nodded. "I don't even remember Max coming to the house."

"Jasmin, what is going on?" demanded Max. "And where did Torie go?"

"She's checking in on a couple of the neighbors. You

and Horst aren't the only shifters affected by whatever is happening."

Torie called to them from the doorway of one of the smaller, thatched structures that sat a bit farther back from the others.

Jasmin placed a hand on Max's leg when he started to get up. "Maybe you should wait here. I'll see what's going on and be right back."

She left the sheriff and made her way across the yard to her friend. "What did you find?"

Torie let out a deep sigh. "Come see for yourself."

Together, they made their way into the simple structure. Inside, there was a large, central room with a crude, yet incredibly warm, hearth made of clay braced against a far wall. An ice box and two hotplates rested on the opposite wall. One corner of the room was dominated by a shaped pile of straw piled to a height of about three feet.

Sitting on the straw was a young woman, her head bowed. Next to her a man sat, his arm around her as he gently rubbed her shoulders.

Torie approached the couple carefully. "Talia, this is my friend Jasmin. She's here to help you as well. Can you look up at us?"

The woman hesitated but was gently coaxed to comply by the man's reassuring grasp. Slowly, she raised her face to look at the witches. She was undeniably beautiful. Her silver eyes had flecks of emerald floating throughout. Jet black hair was swept back providing stark contrast to the golden hue of her skin. But rather than a nose in the center of her face, a curved beak protruded sharply.

Her eyes filled with shame, and she quickly lowered her head again, this time burying her face in the chest of the man sitting next to her.

"How long?" whispered Jasmin.

"She's been this way since yesterday," answered the man. "She's a hawk shifter and can't get back to her human form. But she also can't shift to full hawk either."

Jasmin paced the floor, her head bowed in thought. "Other than her shift lock, has she exhibited any other behavioral changes?"

The man looked down and swept his arm before him, indicating the straw construction they were sitting on. "You mean other than me coming home to find our bed thrown out and replaced by this...nest?"

Torie stared at them; her brows furrowed as an idea formed. "Do you feel that she is a danger, either to you or herself?"

The man shook his head, moving a hand to the woman's head and gently stroking her hair. "No. Not at all. I just want her back to herself."

Torie nodded compassionately. "Stay here. Stay inside if possible. We're going to help you. I promise."

Together, she and Jasmin left them, stepping back outside.

"You shouldn't have made them a promise we might not be able to keep," said Jasmin. "We have no idea what is going on, or how to correct it."

"Can't you just cast a spell and fix all this?" It was Max. He had walked up behind them as they were talking.

Jasmin turned to face him. "We could *attempt* that. But without knowing what the cause is, or how deeply the problem could run, we might actually make things worse. We don't even know if the source of what's happening is magical. It could be a virus of some kind."

"One that only affects shifters?" said Max, trying to hide the skepticism in his voice.

"You were just ready to kill a fellow shifter," said Torie. "Fionna and that woman in there are stuck in some kind of weird half-transition shift, and Elric is rolling around all over the floor playing with Leo. So yeah, something is happening that is affecting only the shifters. And while I don't know what that something is, I do have an idea of what it's doing."

Jasmin gave her a quick, questioning look. "And?"

"I think whatever is happening to the shifters is causing them to revert to behavior that is ingrained in their animal. It's reverting them to a place that is instinctual and safe for them. I just can't figure out why."

"Okay, explain that like I'm in kindergarten," said Max.

"I think I see where you're going with this," said Jasmin. "That lady in there is a hawk shifter. Her husband said she threw out their bed and created a nest. Fionna couldn't stop eating. The way a squirrel constantly forages for food in order to prepare for a coming winter."

"And you," said Torie, turning to Max, "what was with the barking orders? Literally."

He looked at her questioningly. "I told you. I don't remember any of that."

Jasmin snapped her fingers. "It's because you are an alpha. You're a pack leader, used to keeping everyone in line. That's the behavior you slipped back into." She turned and faced Torie. "And didn't you say Elric is being more playful? Max, why would he be acting that way?"

Max frowned. "Elric is a beta. It's in his nature to be more submissive and playful, to defuse situations."

"Well, he's certainly being more docile," said Torie. "That could also explain why he's suddenly so taken with Leo and keeping him entertained."

"Now we just need to find out what's behind this. We need to check in with Emil and see if he has been able to isolate a physical cause," Jasmin said.

"What should I do?" asked Max. For the first time the big wolf had a worried look on his face. "Am I a danger to everyone around me?"

Torie looked at him and placed a hand on his shoulder. "Truthfully, I don't know." She looked around at the small community around them. "I also don't know what we should do here. I mean, whatever it is, maybe it only affected Horst and Talia. Maybe it's already inside all the shifters here and it just takes the right situation for them to manifest what we've been seeing."

Max was nodding. "That could be bad. There are shifters here a lot bigger and more powerful than Horst."

"We need to separate those who have human mates," said Jasmin. "Just in case."

"How do we do that?" asked Torie.

Max sighed. "By being honest with them. It's not just the shifters with human mates, but there are a lot of shifters involved with others of a different species with a huge power imbalance. I mean, I don't even remember what I did. If you hadn't been here, this would have ended a lot worse." He looked around. "These are good people. They will want to do the right thing."

He cleared his throat and stepped into the center of the courtyard, raising his arms to get everyone's attention. The shifters who were in their homes all came out to stand around. By now, word had spread among the community of the encounter between the bear and the wolf and the arrival of two powerful witches.

"My friends," he started. He projected strength and

confidence in his voice, but not to such a degree that it would overwhelm anyone listening. "Most of you know me, but for the few who don't, my name is Max, and I serve as sheriff for Singing Falls. But I'm also a wolf shifter, so I'm a member of your community. I was called out here today to help someone in distress." He looked around, making eye contact with everyone surrounding them. "And as some of you saw, my visit devolved into a confrontation. I am not proud of that moment, and I would like to formally apologize. To everyone here in Emberwood Hollow, but also to Horst. He's a good man and a good shifter. I am sorry for any hurt I may have caused you. What happened could have ended very badly for both of us had it not been for these fine ladies right here –" he motioned towards Torie and Jasmin – "and this isn't the first time they've pulled my fat out of the fire. I trust them with my life, and you can as well. They're here to help." He let his words sink in before continuing. "I tell you this so that you know what I am about to ask you to do, I do not do so lightly. There is an illness, of unknown origin, that is possibly spreading through the shifter community. What happened between me and Horst is an example of what that illness can do. Some of you here are already affected by it. Some may be affected and not even realize it yet."

A murmur of dissension and fear arose from the crowd. Max waited out the whispers, waiting until all eyes were once again on him. "Until we can find a way to undo whatever is happening in our community, I am going to ask everyone to make a hard decision. You can stay where you are, and hope that you aren't affected by this; or you can all separate. Leave one another until this is straightened out."

Again, the murmurs rose, this time slightly louder.

"Where are you suggesting we go?" came a loud voice from the back.

"Into the mountains," Max replied. "Away from one another."

The crowd of shifters parted and a man with dark, exquisite, skin the color of midnight, stepped forward. Everyone around him parted in reverence.

"I am Jad-Athere," the man said, his voice rumbling forth like an advancing thunderhead. "I am one of the first shifters to make the Hollow my home. We are one family here. And now, you are asking us to turn our backs and walk away from one another?"

"I am asking you to protect one another. The only way I know how at the moment," Max replied evenly. The big man stared at him, unflinching.

"Jad, if I may." All eyes turned to the man whom Torie and Jasmin had just met in the tiny cottage. "I, too, have lived among you since the founding of this community. Unlike you, however, I am not a shifter. I'm human. But I'm in love with, and married to, a shifter. And she is afflicted with whatever is happening to our community. And while I will not abandon her, I will take her far from this place until we are told it's safe to come back. I do this for her protection, and for mine. You, Jad, are a mighty jaguar shifter. One of the largest and strongest among us. If you lose yourself to your animal, as we have seen happen today…what might happen to me, and others like me? Sure, Horst and a few others could maybe survive a rampage by you…but the rest of the community could well be slaughtered. It's something that I know you would never do under normal circumstances, but what I have seen happening is not normal. These witches are speaking the truth about the dangers here to everyone." He turned to head back into the tiny structure but turned back one last time. "Listen to them. Those of you with spouses that are no threat, I say go together into the mountains, and stay hidden. The rest, the more powerful hunter shifters…you need to go on your own." With that, he ducked back into his home, closing the tiny wooden door behind him.

No one spoke, but Torie watched as couples turned to face one another, communicating in hushed, intimate tones.

Horst spoke up next. His voice was raw with emotion, and he didn't try to hide his tears. "Today, I accidentally hurt the person I love more than anything in this world. Had it not been for these women, who knows what might have happened?" He turned, looking at his diminutive wife as he reached out and gingerly gave her hand a squeeze. "Though it pains me greatly to do so, I am leaving. I will be back when I know I'm not a danger to…" He stopped, swallowing his words as emotions threatened to overcome him. "To…anyone." He laid a hand gently against his wife's cheek, wiping away her tears, until he leaned forward, and placed a single kiss on her lips.

Turning his back, he dropped to all fours, shifting to his bear form, and ran away from everyone, past the cottages, and into the deep forest that led to the mountainsides.

One by one, the shifters dispersed. Some heading back into their homes to say their goodbyes, others following Horst into the deep woods and disappearing in a forest of green.

Jasmin swallowed hard, blinking back tears.

"We're going to find out what's behind this, and we're going to fix it," said Torie, placing an arm around her friend's shoulders.

"Good," said Max, placing his hands on his hips. "Cos there's one more thing I need you two to do."

"What's that?" asked Jasmin.

"Lock me in one of the jail cells and find some chains to bind me with. It's a full moon tonight, and I don't trust myself to be running free."

Chapter Eleven

"Tell us you got something, doc." Torie's boots clicked across the concrete floor of Emil's medical office as she entered.

He was sitting in one of the labs off his main office, hunched over a microscope. He lifted his head and adjusted his glasses at her approach. "As a matter of fact, I did." He smiled warmly at her.

Jasmin waited a brief second before prompting him further. "And that would be…?"

Her words snapped him to attention. He cleared his throat and pointed to the microscope. "I have run exhaustive panels on Fionna's blood, and I can tell you most definitely that the cause of her condition is not anything from the physical world." He sat back, crossing his arms over his chest, infinitely pleased with himself.

"So, what is the problem then?" Jasmin asked.

He shrugged. "That I don't know."

Jasmin frowned. "But you said you found something."

He tilted his head, confusion clouding his features.

"Exactly. I found out that there is no scientific or medical reason for her condition. That was my finding."

"So, we're right back where we were," Jasmin sighed.

"Not at all. By ruling out any viral contagion, then you can surmise that the cause lies in the magical realm. That's your purview."

Jasmin smiled. "You're right. It's time for Torie and me to do what we do best. As long as we know there isn't a sickness of some type being spread through the community, we can work on using magic to find and erase the source."

Emil beamed. "That is correct. I can assist on that front as I am able, but that is not where my strengths are."

"How is she doing?" Jasmin nodded her head in the direction of the medical bay where Fionna rested.

"No change. I've made sure that she remains hydrated and her vitals are stable and strong. At this point I'm more worried about Glen. That woman has not left her side. She needs to rest, and she needs to eat something."

Jasmin was nodding as she headed for the bay. "Leave that to me."

Parting the curtain, the first thing Jasmin saw was Fionna resting peacefully, her head on a couple of pillows fluffed up around her. The second thing that stood out was Glen sitting at her bedside, slumped over on the rail of the hospital bed, one hand locked over Fionna's. She was asleep in the most painful-looking position Jasmin had ever seen someone fall into.

She walked up quietly and placed her hand on Glen's shoulder, not wanting to startle the woman. Glen looked up, heavy bags under confused, red-rimmed eyes. She recognized Jasmin and attempted a half-smile.

Jasmin placed a finger across her lips and then nodded for Glen to step outside the room so as not to disturb

Fionna. Once outside the room, Jasmin gave her friend a quick hug and spoke in a whisper. "I just spoke with Emil. He said Fionna is holding stable. But how are you doing?"

Glen sighed, her shoulders slumping slightly forward under a weight Jasmin could only begin to imagine.

"Glen, you need to eat. And get some real rest. She's going to be okay. But you can't help her if you get sick yourself. So, I want you to go home, get something to eat, and get some sleep. Once you're refreshed, then come back. And I promise, I'll be right here when you do. I'm not going to leave her side."

Glen cast a weary eye towards the curtain, and then back to Jasmin. "I don't think I can. After everything she's been through, you'd think I would be used to things like this. But you didn't see the fear in her eyes. It's as if she was losing herself somehow..."

"We are looking for the cause of all this," said Jasmin. "And we're going to find it and make things right. We all have people we care about who are being impacted by what's happening. That in no way negates what you're feeling, but it just means we are fighting all the harder to make sure Fionna, and everyone else, come out of this healthy and whole." She gave Glen another squeeze. "And when Fionna wakes, she needs to see a healthy and whole Glen."

Glen let out a short breath and nodded, wiping away fresh tears from her face.

"Good. Do you need me to call you a ride?" Jasmin asked.

Glen shook her head. "I'm not that out of it. I'll be fine getting home." She went to leave but turned back. "You'll call me if anything changes, right? Anything at all."

Jasmin smiled warmly. "You'll be the first to know."

Glen spun and gave her friend a tight hug before

throwing one last glance at Fionna's room. Once she had gone, Jasmin moved to take the chair where Glen had been sitting.

She reached over and lightly patted Fionna's hand. "We have to stop having these vigils, my friend."

She turned her head as someone cleared their throat behind her. She smiled and motioned for Emil to come in.

"I don't mean to intrude. I heard what you said to Glen and...well, your compassion is a thing of beauty."

Jasmin lowered her eyes, feeling heat rush to her cheeks. "I care deeply about them both. And it's nothing either of them wouldn't do if things were reversed."

The look on his face changed. For a fleeting moment, Jasmin thought she saw sadness in his eyes before his usual cheerful and positive smile returned. "Emil, what is it?"

He hesitated a moment, his eyes falling to the ground. Finally, he took off his glasses, letting out a breath. "The way you say that. So assured that someone is always going to be there for you. The dedication to one another that you, Fionna and Torie have. Sometimes, I wonder what that is like."

Something in his tone pulled at Jasmin. "Emil, are you alright?" He didn't answer so she pushed a little more. "The reason I will always have my friends' backs is because I believe in them. And I believe in them because we are always open and honest with one another. There is nothing stopping you from having that with someone as well."

He seemed to mull her words over before looking up, finding her eyes. "I envy you because your world is so full. To be a sprite is...to court solitude. We are a solitary race." His gaze grew distant, and he took in a breath, releasing it in a slow, almost mournful sigh. "Unlike humans and shifters, sprites are left alone to find their way in the world when they reach puberty. We are cast out of the only home-life we ever knew and sent into the world to fend for ourselves."

Jasmin's eyes were wide. "You mean that literally, don't you? That is terrible."

He was nodding at her response. "We are raised by the parent of the same sex that we are. And all familial bonds and relationship building is discouraged. We are taught how to survive from the moment we are born. All in preparation for when we are taken deep into the wilderness by our parent and left there."

Jasmin stared on in horror. "I can't believe anyone could do that to a child. Especially their own."

Emil looked up at her, eyebrow raised. "Don't misunderstand. Don't think that we were not loved by our parent. Quite the opposite. They loved us enough to prepare us for a life of non-dependance. By our nature, sprites are meant to wander the world alone. We are long lived so we will occasionally meet another of our kind in order to propagate our species, but not for companionship. And in the early days of our kind, that was sufficient."

Jasmin waited, sensing there was more to come, and not wanting to pry it out of the physician.

"And I suppose for those of us who shun contact with the human world, those who stay securely locked in the land of the supernatural, isolation is enough."

"And something tells me you aren't the type to shun humans," Jasmin whispered.

"No. Unfortunately, I sought out the human world. I was fascinated by all that it had to offer. I was hungry to learn and to grow. My knowledge of the natural world, and the supernatural as well, led me to science and medicine, where I excelled at both. But it was during my time in your universities that I began to see another side of humanity that I wasn't prepared for. Relationships. Trust. Dependance on another. They were such foreign concepts to me at the time. Not something I pursued, mind you…but the ideals stuck around, planted in the back of my mind."

Now it was Jasmin who hesitated before she spoke. "And now? How do you feel about things now?"

He looked up, his eyes sparkling in the low light. "I think there are people in this human world that I would very much like to get to know better…"

His gaze held hers, and for just a moment Jasmin was afraid he might be able to hear her heartbeat begin to race.

"Oh for goodness' sake, would you two just go out already?"

Fionna's weakened words snapped them both back to reality.

Jasmin focused on her friend, who was lying perfectly still, her eyes closed. "Fionna, are you alright?" She tried to keep any panic out of her voice.

The shifter nodded ever so slightly, her head barely moving on the pillow. She tried to open her eyes a slit, but quickly closed them. "I…I am. I'm just weak. And so very tired." She tried to move around in the bed, but Emil put his hand gently on her shoulder.

"Don't move." He grasped her wrist, pressing two fingers to it as he looked at his watch. "Are you experiencing any pain?"

"No. Not pain…just a weird, displaced feeling. I don't feel like myself."

"Honey, stay still. Emil has you on some sedatives, so that might be part of it," said Jasmin.

Fionna stirred slightly, wincing as she turned her head. "Where's Glen?"

"She stepped out. I made her go home just long enough to eat something and get some rest. I'll call her —" Jasmin started.

"No. Don't," said Fionna. "She's been here all this time. Let her rest. Please. You can call her in a bit, alright?"

Jasmin hesitated, remembering the promise she made to Glen. "Okay, but only until Emil has had a chance to check you out and make sure everything is still good."

"Vitals are still stable," said the sprite. "Holding steady."

Fionna winced again. "Honestly, other than feeling like I've been hit with a hammer, I feel better." She reached up, feeling her dysmorphic features. "But I haven't returned back to my normal human self." She sounded dejected, her body sinking back against the bed.

"You said you feel sore all over?" said Emil. "It could be that your muscles are feeling the effects of your body being caught in a state of flux between your animal form and your human one. I'll add a pain reliever to the meds you're receiving." He saw the concern surface on her face and tried to quickly reassure her. "It's a mild muscle relaxant. Nothing more. I promise." He quickly left the room to retrieve the medications, leaving Jasmin to comfort Fionna.

"Jas — where is Torie?"

"She's taking care of something," Jasmin replied.

Fionna frowned, trying to focus her vision on her friend. "Alone? What's going on?"

Jasmin deliberated for a second but decided to be truthful with her friend. "You aren't the only shifter being effected by...whatever is happening. There are many others going through various stages of this." She swallowed and took a deep breath. "Right now, Torie is at the police department. She's locking Max in a cell where hopefully he won't hurt anyone else until this is all over."

Emil returned, just as she was finishing her conversation. There was a look of horror on his face.

"Did you just say Torie is locking Max in a cell?" he asked.

Jasmin nodded. "Yes. And chaining him in place for an added layer of security. But this is at his own request."

Emil was shaking his head. "Oh no. Have you never heard that a trapped wolf would chew through its own leg in order to escape? Well, that's true. Now imagine what a trapped werewolf will do in its bid to be free." His eyes were wide with worry. "If Max is consumed by this illness, then he will not only tear himself apart to escape, but he will also kill anyone that gets in his way."

Chapter Twelve

"Come on, Torie, pick up."

Jasmin was weaving around the few cars in front of her as she sped towards the town police department. Her cell was connected to the display in her car, and she was repeatedly asking it to call Torie as she drove. Each time it rang through to her voicemail, annoying Jasmin to no end.

She glanced up and saw that the sun had pretty much set, casting the last fingers of golden light across the tops of the trees lining the streets of Singing Falls. That would mean the moon would begin to crest soon, drawing the beast out of the man. Under normal circumstances, a werewolf could either resist or embrace the call of the moon, as they were no longer slaves to the lunar cycle.

But Max had already shown that the sickness, or whatever it was, had made its way into his lupine form. And that was in broad daylight. Who knew what he could do under the sway of the full moon, without the human part of himself in control? Jasmin shuddered at the thought. Afraid for him and her friend. If he did indeed become something uncontrollable, something wholly savage and terrifying, what might Torie be forced to do in order to protect herself and anyone around him?

She glanced nervously at the streets. There were far less people milling around Main Street than was normal, which was good and bad. Good in that it meant there was less likely a chance an innocent bystander would be hurt if things went south. Bad in that it meant the community was sensing something was not quite right in Singing Falls.

Word had surely spread from Emberwood Hollow that something was wrong with the shifters and they could be a danger to those around them. The few people she did see spilling out of shops and eating establishments seemed to be humans. This surprised her. While some of the humans in Singing Falls were blissfully unaware of the community just out of reach of their senses, many were well in the know. And the ones who knew the deal would often look out for those who remained unaware.

She neared the turn off to the police station and took the corner a little more recklessly than she intended, skidding into the station parking lot. Slamming on the brakes, she jumped out, running into the small brick building, eyes open for any signs of a disturbance.

There was a single deputy sitting at the desk, face plastered to a computer screen as she absentmindedly twirled a silver necklace dangling from her neck. She looked up and smiled as Jasmin entered. "Hello, ma'am, can I help you?"

Jasmin reached out with a sliver of magic, looking for, and not finding, any supernatural markers.

Human.

That was smart on Max's part. It was a good idea to have anyone in a weapon-carrying, peacekeeping role, to be human at the moment. She quickly expanded her senses, feeling for any shifters in the building. She only felt the presence of one. A very powerful one.

Max.

And next to him, she felt a bloom of magic, like a sunrise casting its first rays across a dark sky.

Torie.

Jasmin breathed a sigh of relief. There were no telltale signs of distress coming from either of them. She turned her attention to the deputy giving her a questioning look. "I need to see the sheriff. It's an emergency."

The deputy gave her a tepid smile and handed her a clipboard. "Please fill this out and get it back to me."

Jasmin looked at the piece of paper attached to the board, skimming down the very long list of check boxes and waiting text lines. "It's kind of an emergency."

The smile on the deputy's face thinned slightly as she peeked around to look behind Jasmin. "Doesn't look like an emergency is happening."

Jasmin sighed. She didn't have time for this and already regretted what she was about to do. Holding up a hand, she whispered her magic into the air, letting a spell of compliance fall over the deputy.

"Oh, I'm sorry. What was I thinking?" said the deputy, reaching for the security button that unlocked the door between the waiting area and the main station. "Right through here. I'll show you to –"

"That's okay," said Jasmin, breezing through. "I know where he is. Why don't you just stay put and forget I was even here."

The deputy settled back into her chair, returning to the computer screen as Jasmin made her way back into the department. She briefly stuck her head into Max's empty office, then proceeded to the area of the station that housed the holding cells. She followed the low rumble of voices to the very last cell, where she saw Torie in the process of chaining Max to the built-in steel bed frame along one wall of the cell.

"No, wait!" she called.

Torie looked up. "Jasmin. What are you doing here? Aren't you supposed to be at the hospital checking on Fionna?"

Jasmin waved her hand. "She's doing fine. Actually woke up and talked to us for a bit. Oh crap, that reminds me, I need to call Glen and let her know..."

Torie smiled at her friend. "Jasmin, take a breath. What's going on?"

"You can't chain up Max. Emil said that if he is truly not in control of himself when the change hits him, it could trigger some sort of fight or flight response. Like trapping a wild animal."

Torie and Max exchanged looks as Torie took a slight step back. In her hand she held a large lock that she was about to secure the chain closed with. "So what do we do?"

Max winced, rolling his head from side to side as he pinched his eyes closed. "Whatever it is, you better do it fast. Because I'm starting to feel a little, disoriented..."

The witches exchanged concerned glances. "We could just seal him in here...use magic to secure the bars and walls," said Torie.

Jasmin shook her head. "Emil made it sound like he will rip himself apart rather than be caged like that. So, that won't work."

"What if we sedate him?" Torie suggested.

"That might work. But we'd need time to figure out what and how much. Sedating the wolf in him is one thing, but we don't have time to figure out what that might do to the human side. Maybe we could get him far enough out of town that he won't be a danger. Like the mountain just outside Emberwood Hollow where the other shifters went."

"Do we have time to do that?" Torie wondered.

"No. You don't." It was little more than a growl that escaped Max's clenched jaws. He was starting to shake as he wrapped his arms around himself, trying to physically contain his wolf. "I'm an alpha...no matter where you take me, I'll find my way back here. I can feel the shift wanting to happen... but something is wrong with the wolf inside me. He feels...crazed."

Panic was starting to set in. The witches began to debate their options.

"Torie...Jasmin," Max said, "If it comes down to it... don't let me hurt anyone. Just...do what you have to."

"Well, it's not going to come to that," said Jasmin. "With our magic, if we have to freeze you in place until this is over, we'll do it."

"That would be the ultimate cage," said Torie. "If what Emil said is true, who knows what that might do to his psyche?"

"Well, we don't have any time left, so..."

"What if we stop him from shifting?" asked Torie, eyes wide with hope.

Jasmin frowned. "I don't know how we could do that. We could try a humanizing spell, but that could have permanent consequences If we did manage it, we might not even be able to reverse something like that. Shifters are who they are meant to be, they are tied into the natural order created by –" She stopped, a thought crossing her mind.

"What? What is it?" asked Torie, her eyes moving from her friend to a struggling Max and back again.

"Supernatural creatures, but especially shifters, are tied directly to the ley lines."

Torie's mouth dropped. "So, all we have to do is cut him off from the ley lines."

Jasmin was nodding vigorously. "We need something to act as a binder, then block the influence of the ley lines."

"Silver…" Max growled.

"Yes," said Jasmin. "That would work. Pure silver is anathema to shifters! It could help to filter out whatever is happening *and* keep him from shifting. We just need to find some quickly." Her eyes lit up and she snapped her finger, running from the cell.

She returned seconds later with a thin, silver necklace clasped in her hand. She looked at Max. "If this works, you better give your deputy a raise."

The wolf groaned, clutching his sides. "If it doesn't, I just hope I don't accidentally eat her."

Jasmin wanted to laugh but found herself shuddering instead.

"So how do we do this?" asked Torie.

"Well, first, we fit this to Max. Then we must find the ley lines that are feeding him and sever the ties. It won't be permanent, of course, but that's where the silver should come into play. It will prevent the lines from reforming their attachment to him until we remove it."

Carefully, Jasmin approached the wolf and bade him to hold out his arm. He was starting to shift, and she quickly placed the silver necklace around his wrist, wrapping it so that it couldn't slip off but giving enough room to account for any expansion he might experience if he did shift.

"Now, we create a spell that will allow the silver to shield the wearer from any ley line influence." She looked up at Max. "This may be a bit uncomfortable."

His response was little more than a groan. "Can't be as bad as what I'm already feeling." His eyes were yellow, and she could see the change happening in his jawline as it began to protrude and widen, making room for razor-sharp fangs to come through.

Jasmin gave Torie a nod. "We're not going to have time to make this fancy. Down and dirty hex magic will have to do."

Together, they synched their magic and began to chant.

"Let this shifter's essence now be unbind,
may the ley lines sever, no form to find.
Magic of the Earth, hold him tight,
confine his change, deny his might."

Magic flared to life around them as green and orange power surged, swirling about and through the wolf as he howled in pain. The witches maintained their concentration as the backlash of power threatened to overrun them.

"Ugh," said Torie through gritted teeth. "I've never felt anything like this before."

"It's the ley lines," replied Jasmin, focusing on the task at hand. "They don't like being tampered with."

Despite the backlash of power, the witches held fast, pulling at the ley lines, twisting them away from Max until there was only the wolf standing before them. And then, that visage faded away, until only the man remained. He dropped to the thin mattress, rubbing at strained muscles as the witches struggled to catch their breath.

Jasmin looked at him, searching for any trace of the beast within.

"It worked," she said. "He's human. How do you feel, Max?"

The sheriff twisted where he sat, stretching his arms and shoulders. "Strange. Me, but also not me. I can't sense my wolf. But my thoughts are mine again; I don't feel on the verge of madness."

He looked down at the silver necklace wrapped around his wrist. Iridescent energies sparked through the silver, coursing around his wrist.

"It burns a little," he said.

"Then just like an antiseptic, that means it's working," said Jasmin. "But that also leads us to our next problem."

Torie exhaled slowly. "Yes. We found the problem with the shifters. It's coming from the ley lines. They've been poisoned."

"And that tells us who is responsible for this," added Jasmin.

Torie gave her a hard stare. "We need to find Malena and this dark cabal she is working with. It's time to put an end to the Umbrali once and for all."

Chapter Thirteen

"But I don't understand. Why can't we?" Torie asked.

She and Jasmin were sitting in her study, listening to the wind howl against the windows, the night sky split by flashes of lightning followed by thunder they could feel in their bones.

"Because it's risky enough using that spell to free Max, Elric and Fionna from the effects of the poisoned ley lines. To try it on a larger scale, which is what we would need to do in order to impact all the shifters, would be to court disaster," answered Jasmin. "Besides, the two of us aren't strong enough to power a spell that big. If we break something...who knows what could happen? We could accidentally cut off the shifters from the source of who they are, forever."

Torie sighed, rubbing at the back of her neck and rolling her shoulders forward. "I know. You're right of course. I just hate this feeling of helplessness. Of knowing that there are so many members of our community in hiding – in solitude – up on the mountains, and we can't help them."

"We are helping them. We discovered where this is coming from and most likely who is behind it. Now, we just need to track down these witches."

Torie winced at Jasmin's words. The thought of sharing a moniker with people who would willingly inflict the pain they caused annoyed her to no end. "They can't have just vanished into thin air."

"We've tried every locator spell known to us, and no luck. Whatever they are using to mask themselves from our magic, it's potent stuff."

Torie frowned. "They're using our own magic to hide from us. I can feel it." And while she couldn't explain it, she could indeed *feel* what was happening to the town around her. And it was making her sick to her stomach.

"The key is finding Malena. I just know it," said Jasmin. "She was playing us all along. Tricking us into using our hex magic to free her from that tattoo – " She stopped, staring at her friend.

"What is it?" asked Torie.

"Torie, why did she need us to remove that tattoo? If, as Rowena claims, there are male hex witches behind this –"

"Then why did she need *us* to remove it? Why not just ask *them* to do it?" Torie said, finishing her friend's thought.

They stared at one another, minds racing.

"I'd say there's one of two possibilities here," said Jasmin. "One, Rowena was wrong, and they really aren't hex witches. Or two, there are limits to what they can do. Limits that we can exceed."

Torie considered this as she began to pace the length of the study. "Or three, whoever put that lock on Malena wasn't a witch at all, but something else. Something the male witches couldn't break."

Jasmin's eyes lit up. "Eliza put the tattoo on Malena. But maybe she didn't create it. Didn't she say her late husband had contact with hex witches? Who knows where he could have obtained it from?"

"Exactly." Torie was pacing faster now. "For all we know, he got it from a source that is beyond hex magic."

"Rowena," said Jasmin. "An earth goddess could create a binding that no male witch could ever hope to break."

"Yes. That would explain why Malena needed us to do it."

"So, that would mean that if these men are using hex magic, it still has a weakness. We just need to figure out how to exploit it. That could be how we find them," said Jasmin.

"When I was first learning to use my magic, you said that all magic had its limits. That for every spell, there was a counter spell. Maybe we are thinking about this all wrong. Instead of trying to *find* them using our magic…"

"Let's lure them to us using our magic," Jasmin finished.

A light knocking at the door grabbed their attention.

"Hey, sorry to bother you." It was Elric. He took a tentative step into the office, hands clasped in front of him. Leo crept in behind him, peeking between the wolf's legs, his tail wrapped around one of Elric's thighs. "I just wanted to let you know that I've cleaned up the mess we made in the living room and will replace the furniture that got damaged."

Torie smiled. "I told you that you didn't have to do that."

He shrugged sheepishly. "I know I've said it before, but I am really sorry about my behavior." He was slowly shaking his head, unable to make eye contact. "And I remember it…

but it's like it was a dream. Like I was watching someone else doing all that, but it wasn't me."

"Well, one thing is for sure, you certainly bonded with Leo," Torie said.

Elric smiled, looking down at the little dragon. "Honestly, it was fun. But...maybe we'll keep the rough and tumble outside from now on." In response, Leo's wings vibrated, and the little dragon took flight, landing on Elric's shoulder. "Anyway, I'm going to head out for a bit. I'm going with Max over to Emberwood Hollow. We're taking some food and water to the humans who stayed. They don't want to go into town for fear their mates may return for some reason, and they don't want them coming back to an empty village."

Torie felt the weight of his words, and it only added to her resolve. "That's an admirable thing. Thank you for doing that."

He smiled. "Fionna is donating a bunch of stuff from the bakery. Sugar seems to make everything better."

"Hey, you might want to also keep an eye on the humans around town as well. I noticed earlier that there were quite a few out and about considering what is going on."

Torie frowned. "Don't they usually follow the lead of the supernaturals in the community? Even if they don't really understand why?"

"Yes," answered Jasmin. "That's why it was so strange to see."

"I'll mention it to Max. Might be a perfect time for some of his human deputies to be out on patrol. I'll call you if anything happens you need to know about," Elric said.

"Even if it doesn't, call me and let me know how you're doing," Torie said quickly.

Eric nodded and blew her a kiss and a wink before turning to leave.

Leo floated over to the witches and settled on the couch. "El is okay?"

No matter how much she was getting used to hearing words come from the dragon, it still shocked her each time he spoke.

"Elric is going to be fine. Don't you worry about him," she said in a soothing tone. She reached out and scratched under his chin until he curled up in a ball. In a matter of minutes, he was snoring lightly.

"Wow," said Jasmin, looking on in wonder at Leo. "It's like having a toddler and puppy all rolled into one."

Torie couldn't help but laugh softly. "Well, I guess the good thing that has come from all this is that he and Elric have certainly bonded."

"Well, you hope it's a good thing," said Jasmin. "A dragon developing an attachment to a witch and a were-wolf." She shook her head in amusement. "Only in Singing Falls."

Torie was nodding, her eyes focused on the tiny dragon. "And that's all part of what makes this town so special. The coexistence that you won't find anywhere else. We aren't letting some madmen tear it apart for their own needs."

"Agreed. So, all we have to do now is figure out a way to draw them to us."

"Well, what brought them out before?" Torie asked. "Malena used us because they needed access to things only we were able to give them. What if we do that again? Create a scenario where they believe we have something they didn't realize they needed."

Jasmin nodded slowly. "That could work. The problem is,

we have no idea how to even start with something like that. We don't even know where they are that we could begin to dangle a carrot in front of them." She sighed in exasperation. "For that matter, we don't even know what kind of carrot to dangle."

Torie stopped rubbing Leo and looked up at her friend. "Maybe we've already dangled it."

Jasmin focused her attention on her friend. "I'm listening."

"The ley lines. Whatever the Umbrali are doing, it's messing with the ley lines. That could be a byproduct of whatever they are up to, or…"

"It could be the end game," added Jasmin.

"Exactly. Either way, chances are, they will take notice if we start manipulating them as well. Let's say they are manipulating the lines on purpose. What would they benefit from doing that?"

Jasmin walked back and forth a few paces, obviously deep in thought before turning to Torie. "There are the obvious enhancements. Greater magical power, and a near inexhaustible energy supply. Or, the ley lines are connected to the forces of nature, so they could attempt control over the land itself. But that doesn't feel right." She chewed on her bottom lip a bit before looking up. "They could be seeking dominion over other magical beings. By controlling the ley lines, they could control the creatures most directly tied to them."

"Like the shifters," said Jasmin.

"Yes. Or maybe they are trying to awaken something… or grant power to a different type of supernatural. Control over the ley lines would allow that."

Torie frowned, her thoughts spinning. "That's a frightening thought." Suddenly, her eyes grew wide. "Jasmin, if they can grant power to supernaturals, can they take it away?"

Jasmin seemed to chew on the inside of her jaw as she considered the question. "In theory, yes."

Torie stood up. "Could they take *our* powers away? Add our magic to their own?"

Jasmin looked as if she were about to be physically sick at the thought. "Yes. They could do that."

Now it was Torie who was beginning to pace. "So, it stands to reason that if they can do that, then why can't we?"

Jasmin stared in disbelief. "Because it's insane to even try it. Sure, we tap into the power of the lines when we perform our spells, but it would take a full coven to warp the ley lines and actually reroute their power. Because that's what it would take. We would need something – an element of great power and stability – to try and contain that much energy."

"Like a focusing gem or crystal of some kind?" Torie asked.

Jasmin shook her head. "No. It would need to be far more powerful than that. Something elemental. I can't think of anything capable of doing it."

"But there must be something. Otherwise, why would the Umbrali be attempting it?"

"*If* that's what they are up to," said Jasmin.

Torie shook her head. "It doesn't matter that we don't have anything capable of doing it. We just need for them to *think* we do."

"That's a dangerous bluff."

Torie smiled, excited by the audacity of her plot. "But it's a bluff they would want to call."

"I like it. I'm sure we can rig something up. Now we just

need to figure out the best way to leak the word to them. Which should be interesting considering we don't even know who they are or where to start looking."

They were silent for a moment and then Torie's eyes lit up. "Of course! It's so obvious." She gave her friend a mischievous look. "The solution has been staring us in the face this whole time. I know exactly how to reach this mysterious cabal."

Chapter Fourteen

"I hope you're right about this. If not, we're about to not only out ourselves, but probably scare the bejeezus out of an innocent as well," said Jasmin.

"Oh, ye of little faith," replied Torie. "It will work. I'm sure of it."

The two of them sat in the bakery at a small table next to the large storefront picture window overlooking Main Street. Two espresso cups and a couple of blueberry scones sat on the table between them as they studied the people walking along the sidewalk.

Fionna walked up to them, making a show of creating small talk. She smiled gleefully, masking the worry she had expressed previously. "Are you sure about this?"

"Yes," said Torie, exhaling as she sipped at her espresso. "It will work. You just be ready when the time comes."

"And you're sure it's safe?" asked Fionna. "I don't want to ever go back to…that."

Torie looked at her friend, reaching for her hand. "I

promise you. This will all be glamour magic. Nothing will be real."

Jasmin looked up at Fionna. "Are you sure Nicholas and Tara won't be coming in?"

Fionna nodded. "Yes, I told them I needed to do inventory today and that they could have the day off. As far as they are concerned, the bakery is closed."

"That's good," said Torie. Movement outside the window caught her eyes and she quickly dropped her attention to the scone as she dropped her voice to a whisper. "Okay, showtime."

Fionna quickly made her way back into the kitchen, leaving Torie and Jasmin sitting alone in the front of the bakery. They made small talk, showing one another pictures on their phones and each taking turns laughing at something the other said.

They registered the chime that rang out indicating someone had opened the front door but didn't immediately look up. Torie pushed her scone away and raised her espresso cup which allowed her to steal a casual look towards the front of the cafe. Sure enough, the couple that had been milling about on the sidewalk, surreptitiously looking in the window, had wandered inside and were perusing the baked goods on display at the serving counter.

They were both in their early forties; he dressed in a pair of dark denim jeans and a button-down shirt, while the woman wore a stylish skirt that came to mid-calf, paired with an oversized men's white Oxford shirt.

"Recognize them?" Torie asked under her breath.

Jasmin made a play of shifting her plate around and lifting her phone to take a selfie, allowing her a glimpse at the couple as well. "Not at all. Never seen them here in town before."

Torie watched as the couple looked over the goods, pointing out all the sugary goodness on display. They also stole glances at the witches, who appeared to once again be focused on their phones and conversation. Finally, the couple made their way to the register, looking around for any sign of a cashier. The man turned in Torie and Jasmin's direction and cleared his throat. "Excuse me, do you happen to know if anyone is working?"

Torie smiled. "Yes, there's a young lady back there somewhere." She rolled her eyes. "She is usually a lot more attentive. Definitely not on her A-game today."

"Really?" said the man, turning back around. He leaned across the counter slightly, raising his voice. "Hello? Is anyone there?"

An answering clamor came from the back of the bakery. A loud clang of pots and baking sheets smashing to the floor. The man and woman were taken aback, their spines stiffening as they reached for each other.

The metal doors to the kitchen swung open and Fionna stumbled out, the yellow and red apron she wore covered in flour. The couple stepped back as she staggered towards the register, one hand covering her face, her gait wobbly. She seemed confused, head down as she mumbled to herself before making her way to the countertop where she slammed her fist down. She looked up at the couple, her face once again twisted into the combination of human and shifter that had plagued her.

The woman screamed, her hand flying to her mouth as she and the man backed away. Then, as one, they turned to flee the bakery, but Fionna vaulted over the counter to land between them and the door. The shifter adopted an aggressive stance, her eyes dark and threatening as she focused on the couple.

The man took a step forward, placing his body between that of Fionna's and the woman he was with. "We mean you no harm."

"Yes, we really aren't here for you," said the woman, her voice high-pitched as she peered over the man's shoulder.

"Not another one," said Jasmin, leaping from her seat.

"Why does this keep happening?" said Torie as she stood. She slowly raised her hand in the direction of the frightened couple. "Don't worry. My friend and I are going to take care of this. You don't have anything to be worried about."

The couple exchanged unsure looks and then turned their attention on Fionna as she took another menacing step toward them.

"Jasmin, hurry, we don't have a lot of time," said Torie.

"But *they* will see us," Jasmin replied.

Torie raised her hands, calling up a magical glow to shimmer around them. "We'll worry about that later. Right now, we must save that shifter."

"Agreed," said Jasmin, her movements mimicking that of her friend. "Thankfully, we now know how to control the ley lines and siphon off the excess power to make us stronger." She reached into the purse slung obliquely across her torso and withdrew a gleaming yellow pendant.

The witches closed their eyes and began to chant.

> *"Oh spirits of the Earth, the sky and the sea,*
> *we besiege you now to hear our plea.*
> *Give us the strength in this darkest hour,*
> *to make the might of the ley become our power.*
> *Within this gem we bind you true,*
> *so that this shifter can regain her form anew."*

Light swirled about them, engulfing Fionna, drawing energy from her and becoming even brighter, before coalescing into a single ball of power and being drawn into the necklace Jasmin held. Quickly, she shoved it into her purse, snapping it closed.

"Got it," she said. "It's a good thing we found a way to safely harness the ley energies."

"Yep," said Torie. "Now, for every shifter we save, we will get that much stronger." Her eyes grew wide as she looked at the couple staring at her. "Oh my, I forgot you were there. I'm sorry you had to see that. But as you've probably guessed, there is a lot more to this little town than meets the eye."

The man's eyes grew round as he took the woman by the hand, leading her towards the door. "Yeah, actually, we didn't see anything. Right, honey?"

"Nope, nothing at all," replied the woman as they hurried for the front door.

"Wait, what about a pastry?" said a now human Fionna, calling after them.

The slamming of the glass door was her only answer as the couple rushed from the establishment, heading for a sleek sports car parked by itself a few doors down. The trio watched as they peeled out of their parking spot and raced away from Main Street.

"Well, was that convincing enough?" asked Fionna, placing her hands on her hips.

"Oscar worthy," replied Jasmin with a smile. "Now we just have to hope that Torie's hypothesis is correct."

Torie stared out the front door towards the nearly empty streets. "It is. I mean, think about it. You said yourself that there are way more humans out and about in town than there should be, considering everything that is going on.

108

And on top of that, they are people we've never seen in town before. And between the three of us we know almost everyone. Granted, there may be a few out-of-towners visiting at any given time, but not this many. And the fact that Max closed all the hiking trails...that all tells me these people are not just tourists. We were wondering if and how the cabal could be keeping tabs on things in town without us knowing. Well, I'm betting they aren't using magic; they're doing it the old-fashioned way."

"It does make sense," said Jasmin. "If they bought that performance, we just have to wait and see what kind of response we get."

"Hey, you alright?" Jasmin asked, taking Fionna by the arm.

The shifter was clearly shaken and moved to sit in one of the chairs next to the fireplace. Torie disappeared into the kitchen and quickly returned with a glass of water.

"I'm fine," said Fionna, smiling as she took the water from her friend. "I feel ridiculous. It was just...seeing the look on their faces when they saw me; it made me wonder just how bad it must have been when it was the real thing." She reflexively touched her face, her fingers scanning for any abnormalities before she took a drink from her glass.

"That wasn't you they saw," said Torie. "It was all smoke and mirrors. Not the real Fionna."

Fionna looked up at them, offering a weak smile. "But wasn't it though? Who's to say that's not what I really look like? Maybe what I will one day become." She dropped her eyes to the glass now cupped in her lap.

Torie reached out and gingerly lifted her chin so their eyes met. "Because I see the real you every day. And she is beautiful and strong and brilliant. And that's all anyone who knows you will ever see."

Crimson crept up the squirrel shifter's face and she had to look away from her friends as she tried to blink away the tears threatening to spill down her cheeks. "So. What now?"

"Now we wait," said Torie. "For what I'm not sure, but I'm betting it will happen quickly."

"In the meantime, how about the three of us go and relax in the hot tub at my place?" suggested Jasmin. "It's been way too long since we just had some nice downtime to enjoy each other's company."

Fionna's eyes lit up. "That sounds perfect. Just give me a couple minutes to close up."

Just then, Torie's phone began ringing. She looked at the screen and frowned before swiping at it. "Hey, Max, what's up?"

She listened intently, nodding her head along with whatever the sheriff was saying. "Thanks. We'll head right over."

"Oh no. What is it?" asked Jasmin, watching as Torie slowly slid her phone into the back pocket of her jeans.

"Max and Elric are out at the Hollows, and they just received a call from the police department." She took a deep breath, staring at Jasmin. "Apparently, a girl just walked in looking very disheveled, according to Max's deputy. She said she just escaped being held against her will by a monster."

Jasmin was already shouldering her purse, moving towards the door. She looked back when she saw that Torie wasn't moving. "What's wrong?"

Torie took a deep breath. "According to the description the deputy gave, the girl is a dead ringer for Malena."

Chapter Fifteen

"She's in the back. Max said to keep her in the questioning room, separated from everyone else. I don't know why…it's not like there's anyone else being held here." It was the female deputy on duty who had previously met Jasmin. "Also, why is it that he said only the two of you are allowed to talk to her? Are you lawyers?"

"Something like that," said Torie, as they breezed by the deputy.

"Well, hey, don't you need to show me some form of identification or something?" She stood and started to follow the two witches.

"You don't need that," said Jasmin with a wave of her hand.

The deputy seemed confused but immediately sat back down. "You're right. I don't."

Shoes clicking on the polished concrete floor, Torie turned to Jasmin. "One of these days, you're going to have to teach me that little mind-trick of yours."

Jasmin laughed. "It's all in the wrist. Of course, something tells me it won't work on our guest in there."

They were standing at the door to the interrogation room. It looked like wood, but Torie knew it was just a veneer over a reinforced metal door. She understood the thinking behind Max putting Malena in there, but she also wasn't so sure the girl couldn't have gotten out anytime she wanted. With a small push of magic, she was able to override the locking mechanism and swing the door outward.

Inside, the room was barely big enough for three adults to stand. It was dominated by a large metal table bolted in place in the center of the room. Sitting at the table was the girl Torie had both looked forward to and dreaded meeting once more.

The young woman looked up at them. Her eyes were bloodshot, and Torie thought she could make out a bruise on one side of her face. They both swallowed hard as Torie struggled to find the words to express how she was feeling.

Jasmin, however, had no such blockage. "Well, well, well...look what the were-cat dragged in."

Torie shot her friend a look. "Jasmin —"

"No, it's okay," said Malena, her voice tired and weak. "I guess I deserve whatever the two of you throw my way."

Torie narrowed her eyes, giving the girl a hard stare. "Malena, why are you here?"

The girl looked around. "Well, I can't actually go anywhere, I'm kind of trapped."

Torie let out an exhale. "Not here in the cell, but here... as in why have you shown up now?"

"Oh, that," she replied, her eyes roaming the enclosure. "Honestly, I had no other place to go. I figured if I showed up here, there was a chance you would come see me. I was going to go straight to your house…but well, that just didn't seem smart given how things ended between us."

"Yeah, that was probably a good call," said Jasmin.

Torie ignored her, focusing instead on the young woman who sat before them. "Malena, you know we were only trying to help you. Your betrayal hurt."

Malena bit at the inside of her cheek and her knee began bouncing. "I know. And saying I'm sorry won't cut it. But the truth is, I'm not sorry. All my life, as long as I can remember, I've felt like a pawn; something to be used or traded to get something. Well, for once, I saw an opportunity to use others to get what *I* wanted." She clasped her hands and placed them on her lap, trying to force her body to calm down.

"And how'd that work out for you?" said Torie.

Malena swallowed, finally looking up at the witches. "It was fine…until I realized that it still wasn't me calling the shots."

"You were still just a tool of the Umbrali, right?" said Jasmin.

Malena's eyes cut to the witch. "More like a weapon. One they decided to discard once they didn't need me anymore."

"Tell us what happened," said Torie.

"And don't lie. We will know if you lie," said Jasmin, her eyes flashing green for emphasis.

"I have no reason left to lie," said the girl. "Yes, I double-crossed you. There were things I needed that only a hex witch could gain access to. So, I saw a way to manipulate you into helping me. I did that because I thought that once we – the Umbrali – had everything they needed to extend their power over the ley lines, they would give me a seat at the table with them. I was always treated like the unwanted stepchild that —"

Jasmin held up a hand, signaling for her to stop. "That's offensive. There are plenty of stepchildren in the world in loving, functional homes. Please don't equate being raised by someone who may not be your biological parent to being automatically unwanted." She gave the girl a hard look before nodding for her to continue.

A slight frown seemed to fall across her features before she continued. "Forgive me. But as long as I can remember I was the afterthought to everyone around me. What memories I have of my father are cloudy at best; he was always working, but at what, I never knew. My mother always treated me with disdain. I had assumed it was because I didn't inherit her gifts; but later I found out the real reason. I wasn't even her child…how could she have loved me like I was? Instead, I was conceived to be the answer to an age-old conundrum."

Torie stepped closer. "Malena, everything your mother did was to protect you. She knew the forces that were after you. She and your father tried to keep you hidden. They used that mark on you to help hide you from the dark forces that wanted you. Not to imprison your powers but to suppress them, keep them off the radar, so to speak."

"Yeah, well by the time I figured all that out it was too late. I felt alone and damaged. All I wanted was to lash out. Hurt the people who had hurt me all my life," Malena answered.

Jasmin let out a loud tsk, rolling her eyes. "I'd say burning your mother alive was a little more than just hurting someone."

Torie thought she should probably reign Jasmin in a

little, but she was also curious as to how the girl would answer. She watched her closely, noting the look of genuine pain that briefly flitted across her face.

"That was an accident," said Malena. "I only wanted to scare her, to show her that I was really trying to learn elemental magic. It was a spark that...grew out of my control." She looked away, roughly wiping at her face. "I didn't mean it. But after it was done, and I realized she was inside Jax...I saw an opportunity. A chance to take over the direction of the coven. Use its power to serve the needs of the Umbrali. I thought if I delivered them a complete coven, they would see me as more than just a key to unlock what they sought."

Torie pursed her lips, staring at the girl for a moment. "Malena, did they need your power to somehow unlock a way for them to manipulate the ley lines?"

She nodded, taking a deep breath. "Yes. With your help they were able to get everything they needed to make it happen. All that was left was to use my power to open some door to a dark realm...someplace they could then send the power of the ley lines."

"Why?" asked Jasmin. "Surely they must have explained why they would want to do such a thing."

Again, the young woman shook her head. "No, they didn't have to explain anything. They just said that diverting the ley lines would result in a new world order for supernaturals. One they would be in charge of."

"And that led to you being here?" Torie asked.

She looked around, twisting her mouth to one side, as if she were debating her next words.

"What aren't you telling us?" Jasmin asked.

"It turns out the tattoo you removed was there to not

only suppress my powers, but to also keep anyone else from having access to them. When you broke the seal, it unlocked my powers. But it also removed the gate that kept the Umbrali from using them." She held up her hands, frail and tiny. "They stole them, sucking my powers away for their own use. They locked them away, with the intent of using them in a ceremony to open this dark gate they keep talking about." Her eyes dropped to her hands where she was picking at one of her nails. When she spoke again, her voice was little more than a whisper. "Without any magic, they didn't really consider me a threat. Just kind of ignored me. I was able to get away and this was the only place I could think to go."

She looked up, her eyes moving from one of the witches to the other. "I swear, I'm telling you the truth."

Jasmin's eyes took on an ethereal glow as she stared at the girl, probing delicately with her magic. "Well, she has no trace of any kind of supernatural energy signature. So she's telling the truth about having no powers at least."

"I am sorry this happened to you," said Torie. She took a deep breath and looked at Jasmin.

Jasmin shook her head and motioned towards the door.

"One second," Torie said to Malena as she followed Jasmin out the door, closing it tightly behind her.

"Tell me there is no way you are falling for this," said Jasmin. "I mean, this is worse than the performance we just gave at the bakery. And speaking of, we put out that call… and she just happens to show up with some sob story right after? No way that's coincidence."

She was ready to argue her case further when Torie held up a hand. "I agree."

Jasmin's mouth hung open. "You do? Cos I am ready to poke all kinds of holes in her story if I need to."

Torie smiled. "No need. She's definitely up to something. But let's keep this up until we can find out what. We just have to keep our guard up at all times."

Together they walked back into the room.

"Malena, what do you want?" asked Torie.

The girl looked puzzled. "I guess I don't really know. I mean...you two are the only people I know that I can turn to. My old coven..." She paused, her eyes growing misty. "Is mostly dead. The Umbrali wiped them out because they had no use for them after all."

Jasmin placed her hands on her hips as she regarded the young woman, studying her closely. "You know, horrible things seem to follow you everywhere you go. Maybe you should give us one good reason to even consider trusting you farther than I can throw you."

Malena studied the floor and then looked up; her eyes gleaming. "Because I know what the Umbrali are. There are male witches among them. *Hex* witches."

Jasmin drew back, waving a hand dismissively in the air. "We already knew that."

Malena offered her another grin. "Yeah, but did you also know that they and you have a common ancestor that the Umbrali recently located? Someone who the Umbrali intend to sacrifice to whatever lives on the other side of this gate they plan to open. Someone they intend to trade for enough power to completely absorb the ley lines and rewrite the laws of magic in this world. And those new laws, will only include those supernatural creatures who pledge their loyalty to the Umbrali."

The witches stared at her, neither of them quite sure what to say.

Finally, Jasmin cleared her throat. "This common ancestor. Who, or what, are they?"

Malena shrugged. "That I don't know. I only heard them refer to her by name. Someone called Rowena. And apparently, you two showed them where she is."

Chapter Sixteen

"This is not a good idea." Jasmin was speaking in hushed tones as they stood inside the great room of Torie's house. "Going along with her is one thing but letting her stay in your home is something else entirely."

Torie motioned to her with both arms. "Keep your voice down. It's fine. We have warded this house inside and out. There is no way she can get or receive a signal from the Umbrali, even if she is still working with them."

"I'm not talking about them; I'm talking about *her*. Torie, we still don't even know what she is. For all we know, the Umbrali planted her here, hoping we would take her in."

"She knew about Rowena. Even if she's playing us, she knows things that we need. How else are we supposed to get things out of her if we can't get her to open up?"

Jasmin folded her arms before lifting a hand engulfed in green flames. "We do it the old-fashioned way."

Before Torie could admonish her, a scream came from the top floor. As one, the two of them rushed up the stairs and to the back of the house where there were a number of guest rooms. Malena had been given one of the ones in the right wing of the house, overlooking the treelined ridge where the house was built. Both witches rushed into the room, magic at the ready, only to find Malena furiously grasping at the end of a blanket, engaged in a tug of war with Leo.

"What in the...Malena, what is wrong with you?" demanded Jasmin.

"I fell asleep and woke up to my blanket being pulled off me by your dragon. I thought he was trying to eat me or something," the girl cried.

Torie rolled her eyes. "Oh, for goodness' sake. He is not trying to eat you. That blanket is one that he sleeps on. Elric did the laundry earlier and must have accidentally put it on this bed." She turned her attention to the floating dragon. "Leo, drop it." The dragon spit out his corner of the blanket, his emerald eyes fixated on Malena. Tiny tendrils of smoke escaped his flared nostrils.

Jasmin looked from Leo to Malena, her eyes narrowing. "You know, he won't eat you, but he could certainly fry you to a crisp."

"Not helpful," Torie said, handing the blanket back to Malena. "We'll shut the door behind us so he can't get back in. And breakfast is served at seven-thirty in the morning. Don't come down late."

They closed the door behind them as Torie shooed Leo on ahead and down the stairs. "Why did you have to scare her like that about Leo?"

Jasmin gave her a serious look. "Did you see the way Leo was looking at her? He's never like that around people. Maybe his senses can pick up something we can't. Either way, I'm still on the record saying that I don't think it's a good idea having her in the house."

At this point Torie wasn't about to argue with her. She had seen Leo's response to Malena, and it made her nervous. But she had faith in their magic, and the belief that whatever Malena may or may not be up to, she and Jasmin would be able to handle it.

"Have you heard from Elric and Max?" Jasmin asked as they reached the kitchen.

Torie shook her head. "Nothing other than a quick text from Elric saying things were going fine so far. I didn't tell him about our house guest. I was afraid he would have cut short helping Max out and hightailed it back here."

"You're probably right. I can't imagine why he wouldn't want you alone in a house with someone who killed her own mother and tried to kill you as well."

Torie gave her a sideways glance. "You do know I can take care of myself, right? Plus, you're literally living right next door to me. I'm hardly alone."

Jasmin huffed, rolling her eyes. "What? Girl, if you thought I wouldn't be sleeping over tonight, you have lost your mind. I'm not letting that little monster out of my sight."

Torie smiled, trying not to laugh at her best friend. "Truth be told, I was kind of hoping you'd say that."

"Of course, that depends on a couple of things —" Jasmin started.

"Don't worry. French toast is definitely on the menu for breakfast."

Jasmin raised her eyebrows. "I said a *couple* of things. We also need mimosas."

Torie laughed as they made their way to the barstools at the kitchen island. "Well, that's a given. Hey, maybe we can make a morning of it. We missed out on some us-time with Fionna, so maybe we could invite her and Glen over for breakfast. Those kids she hired for the bakery are amazing and will be fine to open alone." She looked at her friend slyly. "We could also invite Emil over."

Jasmin twisted her lips, unable to meet her friend's gaze. "I mean…that's on you. You're the one who has to cook everything."

Torie burst out laughing. "You know, it's okay to like someone."

"Is it that obvious?"

"If it helps…no, it isn't obvious at all."

Jasmin hesitated a moment, letting Torie's words sink in. "You say that like it's an issue."

Torie was quick to clarify. "Not for me. But think about that. I know you better than almost anyone, and if it's hard for me to tell you like the man, imagine how it must be for him."

Jasmin let out a deep sigh. "You're right. But you'll be happy to know that he and I…talked, while I was visiting Fionna at the hospital. We have a mutual understanding and yes…I believe a date is in the future for us. So, if you want to invite him over for breakfast, I won't complain."

"Done. I'll text everyone and let them know. Now that is all settled, what do we do about Rowena?"

Jasmin shrugged. "Honestly, there is probably very little we can do. She made it plain she doesn't want to see us again, and she's already shown she can hide from our magic. If she doesn't want us finding her, then we're not finding her. And if you're worried about the Umbrali, do you think they are capable of doing something that we can't?"

"I don't know. Maybe. I mean, we still know so little about them."

Jasmin nodded and pointed to the ceiling. "Your friend up there knows more. I can feel it. And I got the distinct impression Rowena knew more about them than she was letting on as well."

"Same here. I feel like something is already in motion and we are the only ones not in on it."

Jasmin took a deep breath, her eyes locking with Torie's.

"What is it?" asked Torie.

"I think it's not so much that we aren't in on whatever is happening. I think it's more that we may be in over our heads. It feels like we're being attacked on so many different sides and…there's only the two of us."

Her words caused Torie's spine to stiffen. "That's it. We're stretched thin, with no support. What if that is what this whole issue with the shifter community is about? I assumed it was a byproduct of what was happening with the ley lines, a sickness the community was experiencing as a result of them being tampered with. When I was in the dream awakening, I could see the darkness infecting the ley lines. I should have known something was wrong then. But I just thought it was part of the trap set for me." She shook her head, her tone betraying her self-annoyance.

"Don't go there. What's done is done. Even we can't change the past." Jasmin began to pace, mulling over Torie's words. "And the operative word you just said was *attack*. What they did to you was deliberate. I also made an assumption. I assumed they were holding you to force me to free Malena. And that may have been part of their plan, but what if it was only a small part? What if they were after you all along?"

"I would never have helped them," Torie said.

"No. But it would have taken you off the playing field. Leaving just me to deal with them."

Torie frowned. "Yes. And when that didn't work —"

"They launched a sneak attack on the shifter community. They couldn't divide us, so they isolated us instead. Cut us off from Max, Elric and Fionna. As well as any others who may have come to our aid."

"Divide and conquer. Sometimes the oldest strategies are the best," added Jasmin.

"You know what this means?" A smile was starting to spread across Torie's face.

"That they're afraid of us."

"As well they should be. That also means they have a vulnerability somewhere. We just need to find it before they can find Rowena."

Jasmin was nodding. "And are we sure that their attack on the ley lines was meant to only cripple the shifters? We need to check in with the rest of the supernaturals in town. See how they have been impacted by this."

"Good idea. That's something we can ask Fionna to do. She knows everyone in town." A shadow descended over Torie's features, her brow creasing. "But all of this makes me wonder. If the rest of the supernatural community hasn't been affected, why just the shifters?"

"They are the most powerful members of the community. Strength in numbers and all that."

Torie was tapping her nail on the island top. "Maybe. Well, one thing is for certain; I'm too tired to continue thinking about this. I say we get some rest, get everyone together in the morning, and tackle this fresh."

Jasmin stretched her arms over her head, letting out a long yawn. "You just read my mind." Her arms dropped and she smiled at her friend. "We got this. We stick together, and we put an end to these guys." With that, she was off, heading for the stairs that would take her up to one of the guest suites.

With a sigh, Torie took out a clean towel and wiped down the countertop. It was spotless of course, but the act of cleaning felt calming to her. The repetitiveness of the physical motions freed her mind to work at unraveling the knot of activities from the past few days.

There was something gnawing at the back of her mind. Something she felt so close to seeing. But the more she reached for it, the farther it retreated. The phone she had placed on the counter vibrated and she looked over to see a reminder pop up. She had scheduled her routine dental appointment for the following day.

"Oh, that's great. I bet I'm going to get charged a fee for rescheduling inside twenty-four hours." She reached for the phone and opened her calendar, scrolling through future dates, taking into account that she had no idea when this issue they were currently facing would be over. "If it's over that is. If some horrific apocalypse happens, do I really care about my dental health?" She laughed to herself, but then something caught her eye. There was an upcoming event two days away that she did not remember booking. She pressed on the date, opening her calendar. Her heart stopped.

This was it. This was what had been bothering her, what she had forgotten. She debated waking Jasmin but decided to let her friend sleep. Instead, she retreated to her study and closed the door behind her.

The secret to figuring all of this out might just have been staring them in the face all along.

Chapter Seventeen

The floor-to-ceiling bookcase in her office was overflowing with tomes and spell books from her mother. She had no idea how old some of the books were, their pages yellow and fragile, many of them handwritten in fading ink. But it wasn't just books that she had salvaged from her mother's old library. One shelf was cluttered with an array of paper scrolls bound in silk ribbons and sealed with magic.

She closed her eyes and held out her hand, calling to the scroll she needed. The rolls of parchment shuffled around until one separated itself from the pile and floated to her. She placed it on the large desk in front of the case and whispered the unbinding spell that allowed her to open the scroll. The artifact had the feel of paraffin wax and smelled slightly of vanilla and incense.

Gently she unrolled it and waited for the text to magically appear. On one side of the paraffin was a calendar, and on the other side, a list that ran from top to bottom. She took a look at the date on her phone to make sure she had the right one, and then held her palm over the calendar on the scroll and commanded it to show her the date she needed.

She shook her head, silently berating herself. How had she forgotten this? The date marked on her calendar came from a photo Jasmin had taken at the scene of Eliza's death. The date had appeared in nearly invisible writing that appeared only to her and Jasmin's eyes. A date written in a form of magical, invisible ink. Torie hadn't thought much about it at the time, intending to investigate it later, hence marking it down as an upcoming event on her personal calendar.

But being trapped in a bottle by a magical booby trap had a way of messing with your mind. Between that and the following events, she had completely forgotten to follow up on what significance the date could have.

But now that her residual brain fog finally felt like it was lifting, she was ready to dive in full force.

The calendar on the scroll shimmered and disappeared in a blaze of burning light, only to be replaced with another. This one was dated two days hence. She watched as the corresponding list faded away only to be replaced by a new one as well.

This particular scroll was one of the first ones she had stumbled across when perusing her mother's library. It was the witch's version of a smart calendar. Only, instead of doctor appointments, dinner with friends reminders or anniversaries, it was filled with events that were of particular interest to supernaturals.

Past events had included eclipses, meteor showers, solstices and equinoxes that could potentially limit or amplify the casting of certain spells. It also tracked the natural progression of seasonal changes as well. It was what had allowed Torie and Jasmin to know the proper time and place to harvest lunarwort and other powerful herbs. But none of that was listed on the date Torie had selected. There was only one event happening that day, and Torie stared hard at it, absorbing the possible meanings it could have.

Harmonic convergence.

That was all that was listed as happening two days from now. Beside those two words were a set of numbers that meant nothing to her.

She studied the calendar, pondering what she was being shown. With a wave of her hand, she commanded the calendar to show her the last time such a convergence occurred. The writing shimmered and blurred as time flew by until it once again came into focus. She stared at the date, as the year came into view.

The last convergence was five hundred years ago.

Another wave of her hand, only this time, she asked for the date of the next harmonic convergence. She watched in wonder as time flew forward, this time to settle on a date in the far future.

Another five hundred years.

Torie willed the map back to her original inquiry where she studied the numbers. They made no sense. They were three sets of numbers, separated by a comma. Each set of numbers varied in digits and the print size and boldness of each set of numbers differed. The more Torie looked at it the more she felt the arrangement of letters was too delib- erate to be random. There was meaning behind them, she just wasn't sure what.

Holding both hands over the scroll, she invoked spells of revelation, hoping to force the numbers to show her what- ever secret they may be hiding, but no matter what she tried, no revelation followed.

She dropped her hands to her side in exasperation. "Okay, let's think about this logically. Calendar showing a date and events coordinating to the dates. And these numbers that show…what? Time? No, that wouldn't make sense." Her eyes brightened. "Location. These are coordinates of some kind. That's why a revelation spell didn't do anything. They are already showing me someplace. I just need to figure out how to read it."

She paced back and forth, racking her brain, and reaching back to her high school geography classes. Latitude and longitude coordinates were used to show geographic locations on a map. But those were made up of two sets of numbers. Not three. Why would there be a third set of numbers to show two-dimensional placement?

Unless that was the reason. This wasn't a two-dimensional placement. And it wasn't meant for a map in the human world. She bent over, studying the map again. Maybe her spell hadn't worked because she had asked the wrong question with it. Despite its appearance, hex magic was fairly simple.

All it required was willpower and intent.

She looked at the numbers again, this time, creating an image of what she needed in her mind. Closing her eyes, she cast an incantation.

"By the essence of the arcane,
with eagle's eye, a vision I gain.
With coordinates thrice combined,
a hidden realm I seek to find.
By the will of elements three,
emerge the sphere for all to see.
Envision now, the fates align,
reveal the place with these numbers fine."

Torie opened her eyes to a glowing, orange ball floating before her. It rotated slowly in the air, the brightness of the glow dimming until the globe looked like a piece of shimmering glass in front of her. It spun clockwise, then reversed direction a couple of times, before settling in one position. There, inside the globe, three red threads converged into a single point.

Drawing in a deep breath, Torie studied the spot. "So that's where whatever is going to happen, is going to happen," she murmured. Unfortunately, there were no landmarks around the dot to help her identify the location. She bit her lip, realizing there was really only one way to solve the dilemma. She shouldn't do it. It could end up getting her in a lot of trouble, but every instinct she had told her it was worth the risk.

She cleared a place on the desk, pushing aside the scroll, and placed a marble mortar and pestle next to it. Then, holding out her hand, she summoned the rest of what she would need for the spell and placed it next to the mortar. Finally, knowing there was no turning back from what she was about to do, she summoned the last of the lunarwort from her greenhouse.

With everything in place, she went about creating the base for the dream awakening spell.

With the last of the ingredients mixed into a powder, all that remained was to cast the psychic spell. Her hands trembled as she prepared for the final step. It took all the willpower she could muster to banish thoughts of what happened to her the last time she performed the spell.

She told herself she would be more aware this time; she would pull herself out at the first signs of any danger. Being trapped inside a bottle and feeling your soul slowly begin to unravel was an experience no one should ever have to go through. She told herself she would rather die than have that happen to her a second time.

Once everything was ready, she took a deep breath, focused her will on the red dot inside the floating globe, and sent a spark of power into the substances she had ground into a fine powder. The power of her hex flowed through her as she pushed her power to its limits. Magic flared around her, and she began her chant.

> *"Boundaries of slumber, hear my call,*
> *guide my spirit where it may fall,*
> *into the realm of dreams, I glide,*
> *to magical coordinates, I shall ride.*
> *As my body rests, my spirit roams,*
> *in the realm of dreams, I find my home,*
> *upon my return, with wisdom anew,*
> *awaken my body, safe and true."*

Instantly, she felt the familiar pull of magic as her consciousness was sucked from her body. The feel of falling was strong as the spell moved her psychic self through space, transporting her to the destination she focused on. Despite the stomach-churning rush of light and power flowing around her, she forced herself to keep her eyes open and senses aware. As she traveled, she cast her mind outward in all directions, feeling for anything that might signal an impending attack.

Then, as quickly as her journey began, it stopped. To Torie, it felt like traveling along a freeway at fifty miles an hour and suddenly having the brakes lock up, coming to a jarring stop that made every muscle in your body tense up. The sudden stillness came with its own sense of vertigo, but she fought it off, steeling her senses as she took in her surroundings.

Around her, darkness flourished, the absence of light triggering her fight or flight response. For a moment she was tempted to flee, the fear of entrapment nearly over-whelming her. But she steadied herself, biting back the emotions that threatened to swallow her whole. She reached for her magic, felt the comforting familiarity of it, even in this ethereal dimension. It flowed to her, answering her call, encircling her like a comforting blanket.

Armed with her power, she focused her attention on the darkness around her. There was something familiar about this place. She altered her perception, drawing her witch's vision as Jasmin had taught her, narrowing her concentra-tion until she could perceive things that weren't visible to human eyesight.

Awareness hit her like a freight train. At the same time realization of where she was took shape, she felt something reach for her. Something dark and frightening, clawing at her, trying to grip her psychic self.

She screamed, lashing out with her power against it.

Immediately, she felt herself snapping backwards. Something had latched onto her and was pulling her back towards her body. It happened so fast that there wasn't even time for the usual vertigo to settle in. One minute, she was floating in space, and the next, she was back in her physical body, gasping as she sucked in life-giving air. Hands, strong and warm were holding onto her as she snapped back to reality. She opened her eyes to cloudy vision as she struggled against the hands that held her.

"Torie! It's me, Jasmin! Wake up!"

The difference in the real world around her, versus the magical psychic realm she had just been traversing was like night and day. Shock began to recede as her vision slowly came into focus. The coolness of the wood floor was a balm to her senses. When had she laid down? No matter. She sat up. The look of terror on Jasmin's face was enough to bring her back to full awareness of her physical surroundings.

"Jasmin? What...where am I?"

"You're in your office. You're safe."

Her friend drew her in for a tight hug. Torie could feel Jasmin's muscles trembling as she held her tight.

"How? How did you find me? How did you pull me out like that?" Torie asked, her voice little more than a whisper.

Jasmin's eyes were glowing green, and her magic encircled them. "I felt the surge of magic from your spell. It was nearly overwhelming. What were you thinking? Trying that spell alone like that?" Jasmin pulled away, looking at her friend. Her eyes were filled with a mix of love, fear, and disapproval.

"Jasmin...I'm okay. I found something. The date that was showing at the mansion where we found Eliza's body. It's the scene of something terrible the Umbrali are planning. And I know where it is."

Jasmin relaxed her grip on Torie, still clearly angry at her friend. "What are you talking about? Where were you?"

In Torie's mind, the image she was able to perceive before the astral world around her collapsed was unmistakable. The rock formation burned in her mind's eye. "Whatever they are planning, it's going to happen at Emberwood Hollow."

Chapter Eighteen

To Torie's surprise, the morning breakfast wasn't dedicated to discussing strategy regarding the information she had uncovered. Instead, the rather contentious conversation had centered on the houseguest she had allowed into her home.

"After everything she did, you would turn your back on her?" Elric said, his eyes boring into the witch.

"I've been through this with Jasmin," Torie answered. "And who said I'm turning my back on her? Have you never heard the saying 'keep your friends close and your enemies closer'? She still has knowledge we need."

"But at what cost?" asked Max. He had followed Elric back as soon as Torie had texted that she had new knowledge about the Umbrali and what might be going on. "I mean, you seem to have done just fine discovering things on your own."

"It just doesn't make sense that she's here now," continued Elric. "You guys put on your little show to attract attention, and I'm betting you got it. Whatever you were advertising is what she's here for." His jawline was tight, as if he wanted to say more but thought better, afraid of saying something he couldn't take back.

"Well, she hasn't tried anything yet," said Torie. "And those bruises on her are real. She's been through something very traumatizing recently."

"*She* has?" Fionna's voice was quiet and soft. She hadn't spoken once all morning and now she leveled her gaze at Torie and Jasmin. "What about what we – what *I* – went through? Torie, she tried to kill me. Very nearly succeeded at it, and you're worried about a few bruises on her? I'm sorry, but after what she did, I will not be turning my back on her. As far as I'm concerned, you're wrong; she does not deserve a second chance."

Torie walked over to Fionna and took her hand. "You are absolutely right in the way you feel. I am sorry if I made you feel like I was prioritizing Malena over you. That would never happen."

Fionna shook her head, her lips pressed together in a thin line. "I know that. And I know that you mean well. But she is toxic. I agree with everything Elric and Max are saying. Every instinct I have tells me she is dangerous and out for herself."

The room went quiet until a small voice floated in from the entrance to the kitchen. "*She*...can hear you."

All eyes turned to see Malena standing behind them. She seemed even smaller and more frail than usual, dressed in oversized pajamas and too-big fluffy slippers. One arm was crossed protectively over her body, hugging the other close. Slowly she took a step into the room.

"Sorry. Even in a house this big, voices carry." No one spoke as she stepped between them. She walked up to Fionna, staring the shifter in the eyes. "Fionna. I owe you an apology. What I did was unconscionable. And I don't expect you to ever forgive me. All I can say is I was on a different path at that point in my life."

Glen, who had been sitting on a barstool next to her wife, roared to life. "At that point in your life? That was two freaking weeks ago. And whatever you're involved in now, put her back in the hospital only days ago. And yet we're supposed to believe that you've somehow made a miraculous change of spirit?" She narrowed her eyes, stepping forward. "You're lucky I didn't see you before Torie and Jasmin. Because I promise you, we would not be having this conversation right now."

Malena looked at Torie, her eyes wide and pleading. But the witch just stared at her, remaining silent in the face of her friends' fury.

"Part of me wishes you had found me first if that was the case," snapped Malena. She couldn't meet Glen's eyes, dropping hers to look at the tops of the slippers she wore. "Cos goddess knows if I had the guts, I would have ended things myself. But...I...I'm just sorry for everything that happened. At the time I had my reasons. No, that's not true...I had the reasons of others in my mind. Still. It was my hand that committed the acts that left your friend fighting for her life. And as angry as you are at me, I'll always be madder at myself. But I know words can be hollow. All I can ask is that you let my actions speak for me until you're ready to believe my words."

Fionna moved around her wife to stand in front of Malena. "I hear your apology. But now I hope you'll hear me when I say this. I do not accept your apology, and I do not forgive you. Do what you want with that, but just know, I will never turn my back on you again." She stepped close, until she was inches from Malena's face. "And if you so much as look at any of my friends sideways...I will end you. And that's not a threat. It's a promise."

Tension in the air was palpable and everyone seemed to be holding their breath. Finally, Malena nodded. "I can understand and accept that."

"Okay then," said Jasmin, moving to defuse the situation. "Now that we are past that, let's discuss what we need to do next. And while we do that can we please eat something? Cos I'm about a hot biscuit away from being hangry."

Elric and Fionna moved to the large refrigerator and began removing items while Glen made her way to the large walk-in pantry and began hauling out fresh vegetables and placing them on the island. Max found the juicer and started gathering fresh oranges from the display stand on one end of the island and took out an ornate glass pitcher from the open shelving next to the range.

Torie and Jasmin watched as their friends began prepping breakfast. Only Malena remained where she was, leaning in and then pulling back from the commotion in the room.

Behind them, Emil cleared his throat as he entered the room. "I knocked, but no one answered. I hope you don't mind if I let myself in." He held out a large box of croissants and cheese Danishes. "My contribution. I must confess I'm not the best cook, so this will be the best I can do. Well, that and I can make a pretty mean pot of coffee."

"Emil," said Jasmin, her face brightening. "How wonderful. Those look delicious and coffee is always appreciated. Why don't I –"

Torie cut her off. "Malena, why don't you help the good doctor make the coffee. It's a skill that you will appreciate later in life."

Malena gave her a curious look and then shrugged. "Lead the way, doc."

Emil smiled and gave the after-you gesture to the young woman, and the two of them headed for the small butler's pantry just off the main kitchen space.

Jasmin frowned, turning to Torie. "Hey. Maybe I wanted to learn how to make coffee."

Torie rolled her eyes. "Not arguing with you there. You definitely need to up your coffee game. But the reason I wanted her to go with Emil is because I need to get his take on her. Emil is very dialed-in to the emotional state of anyone he's around. If she's hiding anything, he would probably sense it. Plus, it lets us talk openly about the question you asked. What comes next?"

Jasmin huffed but nodded. "Well, I'm at least having half a Danish while we talk. Care to split one?"

They dove into the box Emil had brought, savoring the sweet, buttery goodness of the cheese Danish.

"Don't ever tell her I said this, but these are better than the ones Fionna makes," Jasmin whispered.

"I heard that!" Fionna shouted from the far side of the kitchen.

Jasmin laughed a bit harder than she should have. "Was just teasing you, babe. Wanted to check that shifter hearing of yours…see how you're healing."

Fionna gave her a yeah-sure-you-were look before continuing to lay out strips of bacon on a roasting tray.

"Okay, but seriously, why would the Umbrali be interested in a village of shifters? Especially one that isn't even occupied now?" asked Jasmin.

"Well, it's still occupied by the humans that remained after their mates left," answered Torie. "So, the first thing we need to do is have Max get them someplace safe until after tomorrow."

"Yeah, I'm pretty sure he and Elric were discussing that earlier. The owner of one of the bed and breakfasts in town is making room for them. Letting them stay as long as needed free of charge."

"Excellent. And I still have room here for anyone that needs it as well," Torie said. "But that's the easy part. The hard part is figuring out what this harmonic convergence thing is that's happening tomorrow. If we can figure that out, then maybe we can figure out how to stop whatever the Umbrali have planned."

"I'm sorry, did you say a harmonic convergence?" It was Emil. He and Malena had emerged from the butler's pantry carrying a combination coffee and espresso maker, as well as a tray laden with an assortment of small canisters and silverware.

"Yes," answered Torie. "Have you heard of it before?"

The sprite nodded, setting the coffee maker on the island and motioning for Malena to place the tray she was carrying next to it. "I must be getting old. I hadn't realized it was that time again."

"What can you tell us about it? Like, what exactly is it?" Jasmin asked.

Emil began opening the aromatic canisters of fresh coffee beans and pouring them into the grinder portion of the maker as he spoke. "The conversion is the magical equivalent of a full lunar eclipse. Only instead of blocking the moon's light, it blocks certain forms of magic." He stopped what he was doing, cocking his head to one side. "Although there are some convergences that can enhance magic as well. Or particular aspects of it. And I don't know which one this will be."

Both witches' mouths dropped open as they stared at the sprite.

Emil looked from side to side, before realizing they were indeed staring daggers at him. "What?"

"And this is something you didn't think might be something we should know about?" asked Torie.

Emil frowned slightly. "I'm sorry. Honestly, until you mentioned it, I didn't think anything about it. The harmonic convergence is something that happens in the magical realm twice a millennium. The effects of it may or may not be predictable." The physician looked disturbed by the conversation. "I apologize if my reticence in the matter has potentially caused you harm."

Both Torie and Jasmin reached out to him, taking his hands.

"No. Don't you think that at all," said Torie. "I should not have reacted like that. We are very grateful for the knowledge you have and are always so free with. I should have thought to ask you about this."

"Emil, according to what Torie saw, this convergence is set to happen at the site of the shifters' village known as Emberwood Hollow. Can you think of a reason why it would happen there?"

Emil bit his lips, brows dipping in concentration. "The convergence occurs in areas of maximum mystical energies. Natural depositories of magic that occur in certain areas. It could be that the shifter village is where the greatest concentration of power is at the moment."

"When you say natural concentration of magic…do you mean the ley lines?" Torie asked.

"Yes, that could certainly be a source. Especially in this area," he replied.

"So, explain to us what the Umbrali could do at this time," said Jasmin.

"Well, during a convergence, the magical energies where it occurs, align and merge into perfect harmony. Meaning, the normal push and pull...the pulsing of the magic that happens as the ley lines are delivering their magic or being tapped into by various beings – yourselves included – ceases to exist for a short time. Everything merges. That's why witches often can't use their magic during a harmonic convergence."

"But that would mean the Umbrali won't have access to it either," said Torie.

Emil glanced upward, debating her words. "True. But that could mean whatever they have planned does not rely on their access to magic."

"What else could it be?" Torie asked.

The sprite thought for a moment, pinching his lips between two fingers as he considered her question. "There is another impact the convergence could have. But...I can't see anyone being mad enough to mess with that."

Jasmin's eyes grew wide. "What is it?"

"There are certain harmonic convergences that go beyond the mere stifling of power. It is said that some of them can weaken the doors between worlds. It's during that time that creatures from one realm can cross over into another. There are even rumors that this is the origin of what we know as vampires. That many millennia ago, they wandered into our world from a shadow realm and were trapped here when the convergence closed." He shrugged at his own words. "But no one knows for sure. Again, tales that have been passed down for eons among my kind." His eyes brightened and he snapped a finger. "You know who might know? Twilight fairies. They supposedly possess the ability to cross dimensions even without the aid of a convergence. Plus, they are the longest lived of any supernatural creature. I'm sure they have lived through many a harmonic convergence. I don't suppose you know any?"

"Afraid not," said Jasmin. "Fairies of any type are few and far between, even in Singing Falls."

Torie took a deep breath. "This matches exactly with what Malena told us about them soliciting favors from a being from another realm. Now, we just so happen to know where the gate they intend to open is."

Malena was nodding along with the conversation. "I told you. They are going to sacrifice Rowena in order to gain favor and power."

"Power to rewrite the laws of magic," said Jasmin, ominously.

"Well, the one thing working in our favor then is Rowena. If what they are doing hedges on her, then they have already lost. If *we* can't track her, there's no way they can either. And even if they do, good luck forcing her to do anything she doesn't want to do."

Malena's eyes darted around the room as she fidgeted with her hands, trying not to make eye contact with anyone.

"Oh no," Torie breathed, "what is it?"

"Well, they don't have to actually find Rowena. She will seek them out," Malena said in a small voice.

Jasmin narrowed her gaze on the young woman. "And why would she do that?"

"They will use the essence of my power they stole to lure her into a trap," she replied before looking up to meet the witch's gaze. "And Rowena will fall for it. Because she is my mother."

Chapter Nineteen

"And you somehow forgot to mention this?" Torie said, the tone of her voice causing everyone in the kitchen to stop what they were doing and look her way. She placed her hands on her head, as if she were ready to pull her hair out by the roots .

"What's going on?" asked Glen as everyone drifted towards them.

"What's going on is that this one just told us she is the daughter of Rowena. The earth goddess Torie and I met in Salem. A fact that conveniently seemed to have slipped her mind," said Jasmin, angrily.

Malena took a deep breath, determined to speak before everyone could attack her. "I didn't know, alright. I had no idea who this woman was until I heard the council talking about the fact that the two of you had encountered her. That's also when they decided I wasn't essential for whatever they had planned. They could accomplish it whether I was willing or not."

Torie studied the girl, watching her body language.

"You weren't willing to help, were you? Is that what turned them against you?"

Malena plopped onto one of the barstools, broken and deflated. "When the magus – the leader of the Umbrali – told me I was connected to Rowena, and that I would be the key to getting her to appear before them...well, I asked why." She dropped her head, her voice falling to little more than a whisper. "And he told me. He told me my father, Clive, had an arrangement with Rowena. For what, even the magus didn't know. But their arrangement resulted in my birth. Of course, Rowena couldn't raise me, and that's where Eliza came into the picture. I'm not even sure she wanted anything to do with me...but she was dedicated to Clive, and I happened to be part of that package, I guess."

Torie swallowed hard, placing a hand on Malena's knee. "Eliza wanted you. She loved you very much, I think."

Malena snorted. "Yeah right. So much so that she tried to kill me while she was in Jax's body."

"I mean...you did burn her alive," said Jasmin, backing off when Torie gave her a hard look.

"You don't know what it's like," continued Malena. "To grow up constantly being reminded that you are less than everyone else around you. To be ostracized because you aren't as capable as everyone else. To always think you're not worthy of...whatever." She cast her eyes to the side, biting her lower lip.

"Of love?" said Torie.

"It doesn't matter. But I thought that maybe I could start over again. Finally knowing who my biological mother was, I thought maybe that's who I am like. That's the person who will finally understand me and know that whatever I am...it's enough. So, I refused to play along with their game anymore. The magus got angry, and that's when they came up with the spell that would strip me of my essence. Now they're going to use it to lure in someone I don't even care about. Or I thought I didn't care about. I don't even know how I feel about things now." She sat there, arms wrapped around herself, not making eye contact with anyone around her.

The silence threatened to swallow the room until Jasmin cleared her throat. "Yes, well that all sounds like you have some soul searching to do. But, in the meantime, you have given me an idea." She turned to face Torie. "We can use her to draw Rowena out before the Umbrali can."

Torie looked at her friend, unsure how to respond to her. "Jasmin, she has no magic of any kind in her. We have nothing to attract Rowena with."

Malena stood up quickly from the stool. "Again, *she* is right here. And after all that, all you want to do is use me as well?"

Jasmin nodded, not bothering to hide her annoyance. "Yes. We do. But unlike that cabal you were with, we want to summon Rowena in order to protect her...not kill her, which I'm pretty sure is what the Umbrali intend to do. Or feed her to goddess knows what kind of creature lurking on the other side of the veil. So yes, I want to use you."

Malena glared at the witch, her cheeks growing crimson.

"Two things," said Torie. She turned to face Malena. "First, we will not do anything without your permission." She turned to Jasmin, giving her a pointed look before returning her attention to Malena. "Second, we won't do anything that is going to hurt you. This is your chance to start letting your actions do the talking for you."

All eyes were on the young woman as she fidgeted, shuffling her feet in place as she opened and closed her fists.

"Fine," she said. "Let's do it. What do I need to do?"

Torie frowned, turning to Jasmin. "I'm not exactly sure. This was your idea, Jasmin. How do we do this?"

Jasmin gave her a mischievous smile. "A spin on the locator spell."

"We've tried a locator spell," Torie said. "She's still able to hide from it."

"Yes, but think of it as a telephone call. She had no reason to pick up. But now –" she gestured to Malena – "We have a new caller on the line for her. The Umbrali were right in that she will recognize her daughter's aura and may or may not come running. But we don't need Malena's essence to make the call; we'll do it through Malena herself."

Emil cleared his throat. "And that's safe?"

"Yes. Absolutely. Magic or no, I'm betting Rowena knows who Malena is. She'll answer…if for no other reason than to see what we're doing with her daughter. Then, we give her a heads up about the impending ambush and… wham bam, she's on our side."

Max visibly winced. "Please don't say that again. I don't think that's how you use that phrase."

Jasmin stared at the wolf and opened her mouth to speak, but then seemingly thought better of it.

"When do we do this?" asked Malena.

"Well, with the convergence two days away…and we don't really know the exact timing of it…the sooner the better," answered Jasmin.

"That also doesn't give Max a lot of time to move all the remaining humans out of Emberwood," added Torie. "And speaking of Emberwood. Emil, do you have any idea how this could impact the shifters? We weren't able to bind everyone with silver."

The sprite shook his head. "They may lose their ability to shift completely during that time. Or they could potentially give over completely to their animal. Either way, it's probably a good thing you got them away from town." He paused, his bright eyes dancing with racing thoughts. "You know, it could be that what the shifters experienced was simply an advance approaching of the harmonic convergence. The way the approach of a full moon can impact the tides – or werewolves – for instance."

"That would mean the Umbrali tapping into the ley lines had nothing to do with their change in behavior," said Jasmin. "But then why would our spell have stabilized them?"

"Maybe it was the silver," said Emil. "Silver is naturally anathema to many supernaturals. It could have acted like a sedative for them, negating the effects of the harmonic convergence."

"Perhaps," said Jasmin. "But if that's the case, we don't know what will happen to Max, Elric and Fionna when the convergence hits."

She and Torie turned to face the shifters in the room.

"As much as I hate to say it, I think to play it safe, maybe we should go up to the mountains as well," said Max. His statement had a visceral effect on the others.

Fionna aggressively dropped the towel she had been drying her hands with. "I'm not going anywhere." She glanced over at Glen. "We've been through so much lately, and if there is worse yet to come, I'll face it with the people I love."

"Same here," said Elric, moving to stand next to Torie. "You're going to need our help."

"Look, I get where you're both coming from," said Max, "But you didn't go where I did with this thing when I was lost to it. I was out of my mind. And not for nothing, buddy, but a wolf lost to their blood lust is a heck of a lot more dangerous than a squirrel." He shot Fionna a quick look. "No offense."

She held up both hands. "Oh, none taken. And for what it's worth, I understand where you're coming from. But I haven't felt the tiniest bit of the kind of flare up that hit me before. I've felt like myself."

Elric was nodding. "Same here. I have faith their spells will protect us."

Max stared at his friends, eyes sweeping from one to the next. "Fine. If you're staying, then so am I. Someone has to take care of you if things go sideways. But you and I still need to get out to Emberwood and get the humans out of there."

"Agreed," said Elric. "If we leave now, we can get there by mid-morning. That will give us plenty of time to make sure the place is cleared out."

"I'm going to go with you," said Emil. "Just in case you need anyone to make up some additional reasons for them to leave. Plus, I've never witnessed a harmonic convergence in person before. I'd like to be there when it happens."

Jasmin shook her head. "That's not wise, Emil. You said yourself you have no idea what this convergence could do."

"Exactly. What if you all lose your magical abilities? What if you somehow become incapacitated? I'd rather be there with some supplies just in case. Believe me, if it comes down to fighting, I have no problem staying out of the way. I know my limits." He gave Jasmin a smile and reached out, squeezing her hand. She lowered her head, heat spreading across her features, but she squeezed his hand back, nonetheless.

"Um, can we at least get a to-go bag?" asked Max,

looking at the arrangement of food that had been growing on the island.

Torie shook her head. "Absolutely not. We've come this far and waited this long. Another hour isn't going to change things one way or the other. Sit and eat. Everyone worked hard to prepare this meal, so now everyone is going to enjoy it. Together."

Max gave a half-hearted grumble in mock protest before sitting down and inhaling a plate of food. Elric was seated next to Torie, and the witch raised an eyebrow when Leo appeared and settled on Elric's lap, happily ingesting the crispy bacon offered to him from time to time.

Small talk led to louder talk and soon everyone was laughing over something or excitedly sharing their opinion about what was to come and how best to tackle it. Glancing over, Torie saw that even Malena seemed to be smiling as she spoke quickly with Emil. All in all, it was a beautiful morning and under other circumstances it would have been a perfect start to a day.

But despite everything, Torie had a feeling what was coming could be darker than anything they had ever faced. Emil's words haunted the back of her mind. What if this harmonic convergence took away the witches' powers? Would she be effective without magic? Could she defend herself if it came right down to it, let alone her loved ones?

She gritted her teeth, steeling herself for the task at hand. She let out a slow breath, knowing that everything hinged on what was coming next. It was up to her and Jasmin to lure an earth goddess out into the open. And then, they would have to face a cabal of maniacs armed with the same hex powers the witches possessed.

Breakfast ended way too fast for her. It meant that it was time to send her lover and friends off. Everyone had a part to play in what was to come, but that didn't make it any easier. Goodbyes were said, hugs were exchanged, and everyone pretended everything was going to be fine.

"We are heading over to the bakery to close up shop," said Fionna. "I'm giving the kids today and tomorrow off. I don't want them in town when this convergence hits."

She and Glen gave them long hugs before leaving, letting them know they would be back in the morning to join them in facing the evil heading their way. After locking the door behind them, Torie turned to face Jasmin and Malena.

"You're not really going to let them get involved in this, are you?" asked Malena.

Jasmin turned to her. "Yes. We've fought side by side before and will do so again. I trust both of them with my life." She let her words sink in before continuing. "Now. Let's head back to Torie's study. We need to reach out to an ancient, powerful being that for some reason saw fit to bring you into this world."

As they walked down the hall, Malena cleared her throat. "And it's not going to hurt, right?"

Jasmin shrugged. "Honestly, I don't know. I doubt that it will be pleasant, however. I mean, it's blood magic. So, we'll need a bit of your…blood. Hopefully just a bit." She looked at Torie and winked. "Torie, we need that silver knife you keep with all your fine cutlery. Be sure it's the sharp one."

Chapter Twenty

"Do you really think these will do anything?" Torie asked, looking down at everything they had assembled for the ritual.

Jasmin shrugged. "I have no idea. But I do know they can't hurt."

"Okay, that's the last of the candles," said Malena as she walked back into the study. "Eliza always used candles with her spells. I still don't see the problem with having them here."

Jasmin turned to her. "We are summoning the living, breathing essence of an earth goddess. A being that is the protector of nature and the earth itself. I think that if we are going to summon her, it might go a long way if we show we are respectful of the woods and forests she loves."

Malena's eyes opened wide. "No flames. The enemy of the forest."

"Exactly," answered Torie. "We want to appear as non-threatening as possible. Let Rowena know we are not a threat."

"From what I've heard, nothing is really a threat to her," said Malena.

"Perhaps," said Jasmin. "But after we met with Rowena in Salem, we did a deep dive. She is the essence of magic personified. But that means that at some level, she has to be connected to the ley lines as well. Maybe in a way that the convergence wouldn't mean anything to her; maybe not. We don't know what the Umbrali know about her. Better to just give her a heads up, make sure she knows you are safe with us and she doesn't need to respond to anything the Umbrali do. If we can do that…we stop whatever they have planned. Then we can deal with the Umbrali on our terms once the harmonic convergence has passed."

"So the hope is that the rest of these items will add to the ambience as well," said Torie, indicating the table before her. "When we start the calling spell, you focus your attention on these objects, remain calm, and keep your thoughts focused solely on her name; just repeat it continually in your mind."

Malena nodded as she looked over everything they had gathered. Gemstones representing the earth element consisting of quartz, amethyst, and agate were balanced against small clay and terracotta pots and bowls containing freshly turned soil, nuts, seeds and fresh flower blossoms from Torie's greenhouse. A bone herring platter with offerings of sage and rosemary completed the witches' spread.

Malena gave a small laugh. "Are we summoning a goddess or baking a turkey?" No one laughed so she sighed and walked over to the bookshelves behind the desk, running her fingers lightly over the artifacts displayed there. "What's all this stuff?"

Torie gave Jasmin a questioning look and only received a noncommittal shrug in response.

"Those are all things that have made an impact on my life, both good and bad," said Torie, walking over to stand next to Malena. "All of these are books and scrolls from my mother's collection —" She indicated the massive collection of bound tomes that took up a considerable part of the shelving. She saw Malena wince at the mention of what she had inherited from her mother. She quickly walked her to the next set of shelves. "And these are things I have started to collect."

Malena's eyes wandered over the various artifacts, her gaze lingering over a set of golden boxes. "What are these?"

Now it was Torie who winced. "Painful reminders of an encounter we had with a couple of particularly nasty creatures. Best not to touch them."

Malena withdrew the hand she had reached towards the boxes and continued walking along the wall, admiring the various mystical tchotchkes on display. She stopped suddenly; her eyes frozen on a collection of seared glass. "Is that…?"

Torie felt her jaw clench and realized she was holding her breath. She nodded, finally finding her voice. "Yes. The bottle I was trapped inside."

"What happened to it?"

"Leo. He was able to break it with his fire," Torie said, her voice little more than a whisper.

"That little dragon did that? Wow. The glass was supposed to be impregnable once the spell was enacted."

Torie gave her a questioning look. "Well, I'm glad that wasn't the case."

Malena blushed slightly. "Yeah. Me too."

Jasmin cleared her throat to get the attention of the two women. "If you ladies are through with your stroll down bad memory lane, I think we're ready to get this started."

Torie breathed an involuntary sigh of relief, grateful to be called away from the remnants of her prison. She walked back to the desk, Malena in tow, and looked over the way Jasmin had arranged everything. The artifacts had all been placed in a circle on the desk, and in the center of the circle were two stones. One was a pink crystalline rock and the other a stone so black it appeared to suck in all the ambient light around it.

"What are those?" asked Malena.

"Rose quartz," Jasmin replied, pointing to the first stone. "It's a crystal associated with love, compassion, and healing. It is used in spells related to emotional balance, relationships, and self-love. In this case, we are reaching out with compassion and empathy in the hopes our call will be answered." She pointed to the black crystal. "That is Black tourmaline. This crystal is known for its protective and grounding properties. It is often used in spells for shielding against negative energies, psychic attacks, or spiritual disturbances."

Malena frowned. "But I thought Torie had this house warded against anything like that."

"The house is warded against all magical intrusion that I am not familiar with. That includes earth goddesses. In order to invite Rowena in, I have to drop those wards. The tourmaline is a backup. Just in case something else tries to waltz in with her," Torie said.

"Okay, it's time," said Jasmin, looking at Malena. "Torie and I will power the spell. You just focus on Rowena's name. That's all you have to do." She held out her hand, palm up. "Well, that and give us a bit of blood."

Malena hesitated just a bit but then held out her hand, placing it in Jasmin's.

The witch lifted her other hand, which held Torie's

silver knife. Jasmin held Malena's hand gently. "Don't worry. I'm going to be as gentle as I can be. Just don't pull away." She looked at Torie and then at Malena. "Ready?"

The girl nodded, biting down on her lip. Moving quickly, Jasmin made a small slit in Malena's palm, just enough to release a tiny bit of blood.

"Now, squeeze your hand closed over the rose quartz. Let the blood drip onto the stone," she said.

Malena did as she asked, her small fist shaking as she forced drops of blood to fall from it.

Jasmin nodded at Torie and the two began their chant.

> *"Rowena, mighty goddess of the earth,*
> *hear our plea, as we gather at your hearth.*
> *With this daughter, your sacred child,*
> *we call to you and your magics wild.*
> *With humble hearts, we stand as one,*
> *seeking your guidance, O powerful one.*
> *Goddess of life, fertility, and growth,*
> *hear our entreaty, our solemn oath.*
> *In reverence, we bow before your grace,*
> *Rowena, appear, reveal your face.*
> *By the power of the elements, moon, and sun,*
> *come to our aid, your will be done."*

The reaction to the spell was immediate and violent.

Though they were inside, a wind vortex threatened to suck all the oxygen from the room. Lightning flashed and the boom of thunder shook the walls, and for a moment Torie feared the house was about to be flattened. Magic surged everywhere, overwhelming in its power as the witches fought to create shielding that protected them from flying bits of gemstones and bric-a-brac from the shelves around them.

Malena screamed, scurrying to stand as close to Jasmin and Torie as possible as the two combined their power to form protective shields around the three of them. A final blast of light so bright they had to shield their eyes flashed in the room, and then everything went eerily quiet. Slowly, shields lowered, the trio looked around.

"Well, that was intense. Maybe –" Torie started.

"You dare," came a voice from somewhere inside the room. The measured calmness of the tone was terrifying, and Torie and Jasmin stepped back, magic raised, as a shimmering rift appeared in the air. Slowly the opening widened, and a figure stepped forward.

Rowena.

She stared at the witches, her eyes bright and silver, her lips drawn back in a snarl. Her hair had gone snow white and was piled high, bound in a crown of thorny vines. "You dare to pull me here with your magics? To summon me forth as if I am some minor wood nymph to be called at your leisure?" As she spoke, her appearance was changing, morphing into something lither and leaner, growing taller until her head nearly brushed the top of the ceiling.

Torie swallowed hard as she took in the enraged earth goddess. "Rowena, we didn't call you here to ask for help."

Rowena bent closer to the witches, silver smoke curling from her eyes. "I told you both I had no interest in your affairs. You and your hex witch adversaries are of no concern to me."

"Really?" replied Torie. "Because when we last saw you, it seemed like something from our conversation bothered you. And I think we know what that *something* was." She stepped aside, revealing Malena, the young woman's eyes large, her hands shaking with fear she couldn't contain.

Rowena stared at her, then let her eyes drift back to Torie. "So, in order to get whatever it is you want from me, you threaten one of my children?"

"No. Not at all," said Torie, dropping her magic.

"So, it's true then," Malena managed. "You really are my mother?"

Rowena glanced at Malena, her eyes losing a bit of the silver heat they were generating. "In a manner of speaking, yes. But not the way you might think." She turned her attention back to the witches, raising a hand. "I warned you last time that we were not to meet again. Perhaps it is time I returned you to the rock, and this time I shall leave you there for eternity."

"Rowena, wait," said Jasmin, stepping forward. "Hear us out. After we tell you what's going on, if you still feel like zapping us into some cramped cave inside a mountain, then...so be it. But do you really think we would go so far as to summon you here against your will if it weren't that important?"

Her silver eyes drifted between them as she slowly lowered her hand. "I'll give you witches this much; you're persistent. What is it that you feel would be of interest to me?"

Torie narrowed her eyes as she studied the creature looming before them. "I assume you are aware of the harmonic convergence?"

Rowena lifted an eyebrow as her form slowly dropped back to its normal size. "If that's what you have bothered me about, then your time here is done, witch."

"The Umbrali are going to use the convergence to open a door to another realm that borders this one," Torie continued, unabated. "And they are making a deal with a creature that lives on the other side of that veil. Guess who they plan to use as a bargaining chip to get something they want out of this creature?"

Rowena drew back slightly, her head tilting to one side as she regarded the witch's words. "How amusing of them that they think they know what they are doing."

"They know a lot more than you might think," said Malena, stepping forward. She was no longer shivering in fear and her voice rang out hard and strong. "They know your real name, Rowena. And that is all the creature they are working with will require in order to entrap you."

Jasmin gave Torie a puzzled look, then turned her head to Malena. "You didn't tell us any of that."

Malena was focused on the earth goddess standing before them. "No, I didn't. Because I need something from her as well. Just as much as they do. And I have more information to trade for it."

"That wasn't what we —" Torie began but was silenced by Rowena's raised hand.

When she spoke, her voice was far gentler than before. "And what is it that you would like to know?"

Malena swallowed hard, taking a couple of deep breaths to steady herself. "Why? Why did you abandon me?"

Rowena regarded the girl, the force of her power receding as she spoke. "Because you were never mine. I committed the cardinal scene that has been the bane of creatures such as myself from time immemorial. I fell in love with a human. Your father."

"Clive," breathed Malena.

Rowena nodded. "And as improbable as it was, you were the result of that…dalliance." She hesitated. The look on her face told them she was remembering something she was not about to divulge. "Keeping you. Raising you. Those were never a possibility for me. Being part human, you would never have survived. I did what I had to, and let Clive raise you as his own. And though he tried to keep your existence hidden, there were certain factions that discovered the truth about who and what you were."

"The Umbrali," said Torie.

"Yes. And others. But primarily, the Umbrali saw you as a weapon…something they could ultimately use. Clive knew there was only so much he could do to protect you, so he sought out an alliance with the hedge witches. He made a deal with Eliza to help protect you. Together, they came up with the magical seal that not only bound your powers, but also hid you from detection by any other means of magic."

Malena rubbed at her arm self-consciously. "The tattoo Eliza put on me."

"As it turned out, they didn't really need to be able to detect what you were. In the long run, you sought them out," said Jasmin, glancing Malena's way.

Malena opened her mouth to answer but was cut off by Rowena. "That wasn't her fault. How could she have known who and what she truly was? The Umbrali staged an attack on Clive and Eliza, causing them to split up, with Eliza taking sole custody of Malena, hoping that keeping her close inside a hedge witch coven would be her best shot at protection." She turned her attention to Torie and Jasmin. "Eventually, with Eliza's death, her power would have found its way free of the tattoo lock. Your intervention shortened that time frame."

"We had no idea," said Torie.

Rowena sighed. "Everything happens for a reason. Dwelling on the past can only create havoc for the future. All we can do is focus on what must be done now."

"And that is?" asked Jasmin.

"Dealing with these Umbrali. They are obviously more dangerous than I gave them credit for," said Rowena.

"And then what?" asked Malena. "Does that mean that you...that maybe we could..."

Rowena cocked her head to one side as she stared at the girl. "I am sorry. But there is no we. It simply cannot be. The places I must traverse are not for one such as you. Your place is here, in this realm."

Malena sucked in a breath, biting down on her lip as she stared at the earth goddess. Eyes that threatened to spill over with tears suddenly hardened. "I knew it. You're no different from anyone else in my life. They were right about you."

Torie stepped forward. "Malena, stop this. We need –"

Malena stepped away from the witch, turning on her with a sneer. "What I need is for everyone to stop telling me what to do." Her anger boiled over into dangerous territory. "But you'll be sorry. You all will, when the Umbrali seal you two off from your powers permanently."

Jasmin gasped. "Malena, what are you talking about?"

Malena turned to her, a look of hatred spreading across her features. "You should have trusted your instincts."

Before anyone could stop her, she reached into her pocket and withdrew something dark and shiny. Torie's eyes widened as she recognized the shards from the bottle she had been contained within. She glanced to the wall unit and saw that they were missing from where she had left them.

Before she could stop the woman, Malena threw the shards at Rowena.

"Arithiel-Ni-Amura, I call your name. Let your essence be bound!" she cried.

The shards struck Rowena, accompanied by a sizzling

sound and wisps of steam where they made contact with the earth goddess. Rowena moved to act, but stopped, arms raised, eyes focused, as she was frozen mid-motion. For all intents and purposes, she had become a living statue, the shards of glass embedded in various parts of her body.

"It won't hold her for long," Malena said. "Hurry!"

Torie's magic flared awake, golden-orange halos forming around her clenched fists. "Malena, stop this! What are you talking about?"

The girl wheeled on her, hissing. "I wasn't talking to *you.*"

Too late, Torie realized what had happened. She reached out, feeling for the wards that were dropped in order to summon Rowena. She attempted to raise them but knew it was too late. The darkness that invaded her home was both violent and familiar. The touch of blackness called to her, like an old, unwelcome friend, as it brushed by to swarm around Malena and Rowena, forming a cloud of ash-colored mist and dark flashes of light.

The air in the room groaned as the darkness flared outward, swirling around the young woman and the earth goddess. It enveloped them, wrapping them in a tight, evil hug, before folding in on itself, disappearing in a collapsing rush of smoke, taking the two figures with them.

Chapter Twenty-One

Torie and Jasmin stood in the center of Torie's study. The sudden silence that surrounded them seemed deafening.

"You okay?" asked Jasmin.

"Yeah. You?"

Jasmin smiled mischievously. "Oh yeah. Let's do this."

Making their way to the large desk, Jasmin swept aside the various offerings they had arranged there, while Torie removed one of the rolled-up pieces of paper from her bookshelf. Opening it, she placed a map of Singing Falls on the desktop.

Jasmin focused on the red quartz and whispered an incantation. Her magic lifted the gem into the air, spinning rapidly as the power infused it. She maneuvered the stone until it hovered over the map Torie had just spread out. Then she focused her will and spoke aloud.

"Object enchanted, vision entwined,
guide my sight, as I seek to find,
the one I search for, lost or near,

reveal their presence, make it clear."

The piece of quartz spun rapidly in midair before slamming to a stop, a single ray of ruby light shining in a pinpoint onto the map.

"That was a brilliant idea," Torie said. "Getting a drop of Malena's blood to lock onto her. Now we can track her no matter where she goes; even if magic is shielding her."

Jasmin smiled. "It was almost as good as you letting her know we had to drop all the wards around the house to perform that summoning spell."

Torie shrugged. "I admit, the touch of that same darkness rushing at me made me question the decision momentarily. Still, I was shocked at how easily she was able to capture Rowena. I wasn't expecting her to use those glass fragments in that way. How did she hide her magic from us so well?"

Jasmin was shaking her head. "No idea. It could have been anything creating a blind spot around her. But you were right; eventually, she showed her true self." She stared at the map. "And now we know where she is and where the Umbrali are as well."

"Where is that?" Torie asked, pointing to an area on the map.

Jasmin studied the map. "There's nothing there. I mean, other than an old real estate development that for some reason never took off. I think they built a few modern houses there but couldn't get enough residents interested enough to buy. Way overpriced and not a style that seemed to fit the community."

"In other words, the perfect place for a shadow cabal to operate from without attracting attention." Torie took out her phone, flicking quickly at the screen and waiting for the voice on the other end to pick up. "Elric. We found them. Tell Max to head over to a place called –" She glanced over at Jasmin.

"Hemingway Estates," said Jasmin, leaning forward.

"That's where they are now. We're headed out as well and will meet you outside the perimeter. They have Rowena, so don't go storming in until we get there."

"You got it," came the reply. "I guess your plan worked, huh?"

"Better than we expected," she replied. "See you soon."

After hanging up, they hurried to the mudroom and pulled on shoes before racing from the house. Torie tossed the keys to her dark SUV to Jasmin. "You drive. I'll call Fionna, have her go to Emberwood Hollow to make sure Emil is okay since Max and Elric won't be there."

"Good idea," Jasmin replied, sliding behind the wheel.

In moments, they were heading down the road away from their homes and towards a section of town not far from the campgrounds that led to the falls for which the town was named.

"Jasmin, what do you think Malena meant by saying the Umbrali were planning to strip our powers?"

"Well, there's only one way that could be interpreted. Literally."

Torie sat back in the plush leather seat. "That's what I was afraid of."

Jasmin tightened her grip on the steering wheel. "Well, it's not coming to that. We still have hours to go until midnight. That's the earliest the convergence can happen. That gives us plenty of time to take these guys out."

Torie glanced out the window, not wanting her friend to pick up on her fear. They had fought other supernaturals before, even other witches. But they had never faced an adversary with hex magic similar to their own. And if they had the ability to capture and contain a being as powerful as Rowena, they weren't to be taken lightly.

The drive was quick, and as expected there was no traffic on the roads. Torie briefly wondered where all the spies the Umbrali had been using throughout town had vanished to, but then thought that some questions might be best unanswered. Still, as the big vehicle whizzed past closed shops and deserted streets, she could feel a strong sense of relief flooding her. The less the community members were out, the less the chances of them being collateral damage in whatever was to come.

Jasmin eased the SUV onto a bumpy, overgrown street that was little more than a trail, and after about a hundred yards, cut the lights and engine. "The entrance to the development is just ahead, around the bend. We go any closer and whoever is in there will know."

Together, they left the car and made their way farther along the trail, opting to cut over into the cover of the undergrowth when they were able to make out two large brick pillars flanking the street. Beyond them, Torie could just make out the hulking forms of massive mansions cut into the hillside.

"What in the world?" Torie wondered aloud. "Who built this? These house styles are all over the place. I mean, I thought our houses were large, but they're practically cozy compared to these monstrosities."

"Yeah, it was the era of the McMansion, and just before the real estate crash. A bunch of developers pooled their resources and thought they were creating the next *it* place to live for the ultra-wealthy. From what I heard; everyone lost their shirts on the deal. So, the few houses that were built here just sat empty."

"Not all of them are empty," Torie replied, indicating one of the homes with a point of her chin.

The house in question was a large modern style, square corners, concrete and glass exterior set at right angles.

"What do you notice about the place?" Torie asked.

Jasmin stared, narrowing her eyes. "The windows are covered from within. And…unless I'm missing something, there are no signs of security monitoring."

"Exactly. I also don't see any guards." With a gesture, Torie snaked a tendril of magic forward, recalling it almost immediately. "Some kind of weird, low-level wards. This is definitely the right place."

"We've already scouted around back. No guards back there either."

Both Torie and Jasmin let out a sharp squeak at the voice that materialized behind them. Spinning around, they came face to face with Max and Elric.

"Don't do that," Jasmin huffed. "You almost scared me to death. Somebody needs to put a bell on you two."

"And if you did that, we wouldn't be very good at doing our job, now would we?" continued Max.

Both Jasmin and Torie rolled their eyes.

"Is there a way in from the back?" Torie asked.

Elric nodded. "There's a second-floor balcony with some patio doors that look pretty brittle. We can easily get those open. Do you have any idea where inside the house Rowena is being held?"

"No. We just know that's the location where Malena is. Which means that has to be where they have Rowena as well. Once we are inside, we should be able to pinpoint Malena," Torie answered.

Max's nose flared slightly. "There's some kind of magic around the house. Can you get us through it?"

"We should be able to cut a hole in that ward without setting off any other alarms," said Jasmin. "If we can slip in undetected, maybe we can catch these guys unaware."

"Or, how about if we try sneaking in, free Rowena, and get back out with no one being the wiser," said Elric.

Torie shook her head sharply. "No. Not this time. We need to confront them about what is going on. I just don't want to risk another's life doing that." She headed towards the side of the house, keeping to the shadows. "Come on. Show us where these patio doors are you saw."

Together, the group made their way around to the back of the house. Whereas the front looked like it had been maintained to a degree, the back was the complete opposite. The once-impressive architectural marvel now stood as a somber reminder of its former glory. The structure, once characterized by sleek lines and innovative design, had succumbed to their ravages of time and neglect, having fallen prey to abandonment and decay. Vines and creeping plants had begun to snake their way up the walls, finding purchase in the fissures and gaps that formed in the mansion's once-smooth exterior. The backyard, meant to be meticulously landscaped and maintained, resembled an untamed wilderness as overgrown grass and weeds dominated as far as the eye could see.

Shadows danced across the crumbling structure, giving the mansion an eerie, almost sinister appearance. They could almost hear the groaning and creaking of the decaying structure as the night wind brushed against it.

The second-floor balcony jutted outward, supported by the arched, stone opening that led to a dark, cracked, covered patio.

"It would be easier to go through the bottom," said Torie, nodding at the patio.

"There is no opening there," said Elric. "Unless your senses can perceive something ours could not. The door there seems to be bricked up from the inside. But because of the wards we couldn't get close enough to take a good look."

Torie shook her head. "No. I trust your senses. But it makes me think that if they have a basement level completely bricked up with no way out −"

Elric was nodding. "It would be the perfect place to keep someone hostage."

"Okay, first things first," said Jasmin. She stepped forward, stretching forth both hands and brought her palms together. Then, eyes closed, lips invoking a silent incantation, she stabbed forward, and slowly moved her hands in a vertical motion, from ground to sky.

"Yes, that's it," said Torie, her eyes glowing orange as she saw something happening that the wolves could not see. She reached behind her with an outstretched hand. "Hold onto me as we go through." The wolves did as they were told, each placing their hand on Torie's arm as she squeezed through the splits in the warding Jasmin had created.

Inside the opening put them within a few feet of the patio and everyone stood very still. The wolves tuned their senses for any signs that the group had been detected, while the witches used their magic to scan for mystical signatures that could indicate they had been found out. Satisfied they were still not being observed, Torie nodded, looking up at the balcony.

"Now, how do we get up there?" she asked.

"If I could still shift into a wolf, I could jump us up there," Elric said. He looked disapprovingly at the silver Torie had placed around his wrist to protect him from the effects of the harmonic convergence's approach.

"No. It's bad enough you and Max were still able to access your wolf-like senses. We can't risk you shifting as well," Torie answered.

"Leave this to me," said Jasmin. She stooped down, placing both hands flat on the ground. Magic swelled within her as she reached deep into the earth, using her power to call to vegetation that grew wild all around them. The ground rumbled slightly as massive vines pushed upward, snaking from the ground, along the wall, stretching for the balcony landing. Once settled, they formed a twisted walkway, complete with foot and hand holds for climbing.

Elric gave Jasmin an approving nod. "Impressive."

"Let's go," she said. One at a time, they made their way up the large vines. Max and Elric went first, one keeping watch while the other helped the witches up and over the guardrail and onto the balcony landing.

They turned and faced the doors. The frames had long lost black paint coating them. A couple of panes were broken, and the handle hung at an awkward angle. Slowly, Torie stepped forward and pushed at one of the doors.

With a creak, it opened inward, to a space filled with blackness. Calling to her magic, Torie led the way as they stepped from the chilling outdoors into the even colder darkness before them.

They stepped forward just as black shadows started to move around them. A disembodied voice floated to their ears.

"You didn't have to do all that. You could have just walked up and rang the front doorbell. We would have let you in."

Chapter Twenty-Two

Magic flared to life as Torie and Jasmin summoned their power, bringing it up protectively around themselves and the wolves.

A low chuckle came from the shadows. "Oh please. There's no need for that. We're all family here, after all."

Jasmin laughed. "I don't know what kind of family you are used to, but we don't hide in the shadows. Why don't you show yourself?"

The shadows boiled, flexing around the witches before receding. They transformed from a dark, nebulous cloud, to crazy vapor that spread along the floor. And from that vapor, figures rose.

Tall, lean, menacing, and cloaked in black. They regarded the witches silently beneath drawn hoods.

Torie looked around, seeing a half-dozen forms surrounding them. Her magic pulsed as she reached out with it, entwining it with Jasmin's. They were in sync, their power pulsing together and ready for whatever the Umbrali might throw at them. Torie allowed a single tendril of magic to snake forward; a feeler that eased its way into the mist surrounding them.

Another voice, identical to the one that had been speaking to them, floated to their ears. Only this time, it came from a different position in the room. This one came from their right side. "There really is no need for that, Ms. Bliss. If you're putting out feelers for Malena, she's here."

Torie stiffened but raised her chin defiantly. "And what about Rowena?"

"Where one is so goes the other," came the voice, this time from their left.

"We only came here to talk. We need to know that our friend is okay," Torie said. She looked at Jasmin and gave her a slight, almost imperceptible nod. Jasmin returned the gesture, her eyes taking on the faintest hint of green magic.

"Friend? What friend are you referring to? The one who has betrayed you multiple times, or the one who doesn't care in the least what happens in the realm of humans?" This time the voice bounced from one part of the space to another, as if each member of the Umbrali were speaking one word of the sentence, but all with the same voice.

"And who do we have the honor of speaking with?" asked Torie, looking around.

No one moved, but the collective voice rang out strong and loud. "You know who we are, sisters. Just as we all know you; the infamous hex witches of Singing Falls."

Torie's phone buzzed in her back pocket, and she felt Jasmin's magic carefully reach in and retrieve it. Max and Elric closed around her, shielding Jasmin briefly from view.

"It's just that…I'd like to know a little more about you. Brothers. If we are indeed from the same family tree, don't you think there are things we might want to discuss? Maybe we have the same interests and could help you in regards to the ley lines." She stopped, waiting for the voice to respond. Even though it was disembodied, she sensed hesitation. "I mean, that is what you're ultimately after, right? Complete dominion over the ley lines? Cutting all other magic practitioners off completely?" She let that dangle in the air. "Excuse me, I need to check this." She looked at the screen of her phone that Jasmin floated in front of her.

"The arrogance," the voice said. "That you stand here facing death, and you...take a call?"

Torie smiled as she reached for her phone, sliding it back into her pocket. "You see, that's just it. I don't think we're in any danger whatsoever. At least not from you lot."

With a wave of their hands, she and Jasmin dropped the magical shields that warded them.

"I know smoke and mirrors when I see them," Torie said, her eyes blazing orange as she reached out with her power, shoving aside the mist and vapor that clung to the Umbrali. "Tell me, *brothers*, what would you do if Jasmin and I decided to attack you right now?" She half turned and motioned to Max and Elric. "Or what if we simply let our friends shift into their wolf forms and have at you?" She gave Elric a nod.

The wolf advanced aggressively on the two closest figures. Immediately, they stepped back, shrinking at Elric's advance.

"I knew it," said Jasmin "You aren't Umbrall. Who are you?"

One of the cloaked figures stepped forward. "What gave us away?" This time, the voice matched the speaker, and Torie frowned, trying to place the familiarity of it.

"First, I don't see the Umbrali being quite so chatty," answered Jasmin. "Second, the real Umbrali would have known Elric can't shift into his werewolf form until after the harmonic convergence. So, again, who are you?"

The figure reached up and pushed back the hood of the robe. Jasmin let out a deep sigh, slowly shaking her head. "Michael. Should have guessed."

The hedge witch smiled at her.

Torie looked around at the remaining cloaked figures. "Let me guess...the rest of Eliza's coven. I thought you all had been killed."

"Can't believe everything you see," said Michael. "A little blood here and there, some staged carnage. Your wolves weren't very thorough in following up on what could have happened. Otherwise, they would have realized the whole thing was staged."

Max shrugged. "You're assuming we cared enough about what happened to you lot that it would have warranted our time."

Michael gave him a sharp look before turning his attention once again to the witches. "What you do to us won't matter. Soon, you won't be the only ones with access to hex magic."

Jasmin huffed. "Is that what they told you? That soon you would be, what? Upgraded? Cos I guarantee they were lying."

"You don't know what you're talking about," Michael said, his fists clenched at his sides.

"Use your brain, Michael. Do you really think they care about hedge witches? I mean, they're using you to keep us distracted. That's what they think of you. You're not at their side in Emberwood as they prepare to pull off the biggest magical con of the century," said Torie. "Yet somehow, they're going to factor you into the new hierarchy they are trying to create? Come on, man." She stared daggers at him. "And yes, we know where they really are at this moment. That call I got was from a friend who's there. He has eyes on them and Malena. I'll give it to them, getting her there without pinging the blood tracker we created from her was masterful. But now that we're onto them, there's only one thing to do."

There were murmurs spreading around the room as the cloaked members of Eliza's old coven removed their hoods, speaking in quiet, animated whispers with one another.

"We're leaving," said Torie, turning her back on Michael and the rest of the coven. "We have real enemies to deal with."

"Stop!" said Michael, his voice rising. "You're not getting inside our minds with your lies, and you're not going anywhere." He signaled the coven, and as one they all retrieved wooden branches from inside their robes. The tips of the branches began to glow as they pointed them at Torie and Jasmin. "I've waited a long time for this."

"Honestly, we do not have time to play," said Jasmin.

Her power was linked with Torie's in perfect sync. With a wave of their arms, power flared outward as they generated a bubble of pure magic. Will and intent became one as they sent the walls of the bubble flexing outward, sweeping up the members of the coven and sending them flying in all directions. The thuds of bodies striking walls echoed in the darkness, and in the blink of an eye, the battle was over.

Jasmin turned to Max. "Anything?"

The werewolf tilted his head to one side, his nostrils flaring. "They're out."

"Should we sweep the house?" Elric said. "There could be more of them here."

"No," said Torie. She had already turned to lead them back through the patio doors. "It doesn't matter if there are.

This was meant to be a distraction, nothing more. We need to get to Emberwood as quickly as possible."

"That's a good hour's drive from here," said Max. "Maybe more."

Torie glanced at Jasmin, her look anxious yet determined. "It's a risk."

Jasmin nodded. "Yes, but is it a bigger risk to try driving out there and giving the Umbrali a full hour to do who knows what? An hour from now puts us arriving after midnight. If the convergence starts at midnight, we have no idea if we'll have our magic or not."

"But if you don't have your magic, doesn't that mean the Umbrali won't have theirs either?" said Elric.

"It does," answered Torie. "But it gives them all the time in the world to cast whatever spell they have in mind to reach out to this creature they are going to offer Rowena up to. We need to act."

Jasmin took a deep breath, her eyebrows dropping as she reached for her phone. She swiped at the screen, then placed it to her ear. "Okay. We're going to do it. Everything in place?" She listened silently before closing the phone and nodding at Torie. "Emil said it's in place."

Max and Elric exchanged worried looks.

"What's in place? What are you going to do?"

They were out on the balcony now and Torie turned to the wolves. "We are going to attempt a spell that will teleport all of us to Emberwood. We've done them before when it was just the two of us, but we've never tried carrying passengers."

Max looked about nervously at his friends. "Is it dangerous?"

Jasmin lifted her shoulders. "I mean, the worst, is that we drop you, or overshoot Emberwood and end up in the middle of a lake or something. Carrying the two of you adds a different element to casting. But we don't really have a choice."

"What if you went without us?" suggested Max. "We can get there very quickly in wolf form."

"No!" cried Torie. "Absolutely not. This close to the possible start of the harmonic convergence, who knows what effect it could have on you? And staying here isn't an option." She gave Jasmin another quick glance. "We need you for the second part of the plan."

Elric took in a deep breath. "We're with you. And we have complete faith in your power. What do you need us to do?"

Torie took his hand and motioned for Jasmin and Max to come stand next to them. "Join hands and hold on tight."

They held hands tightly, forming a circle. Torie and Jasmin lifted their faces to the heavens, eyes glowing as they sang out in unison.

> *"Boundaries of time, of space unwind,*
> *open the path, that no obstacle may bind.*
> *From here to there, in the blink of an eye,*
> *on the wings of the wind, we yearn to fly.*
> *As quick as thought, as light as air,*
> *we call upon our magic fair.*
> *By the might of elements, air, fire, and sea,*
> *as we will it, so must it be "*

Their magic erupted in a staggering display of light and thunder, as green and orange tendrils swirled about them. Light flared and the heavens seemed to split, sucking the group skyward, leaving only a burned patch of concrete to mark their passing.

Chapter Twenty-Three

The sudden appearance of a swirling maelstrom of shimmering energy in the woods just outside Emberwood Hollow startled a flock of roosting birds, sending them off into the night sky. The magic pulsed with an ethereal glow, casting an otherworldly light on the dense foliage, turning the usually dark forest into an eerie tableau. The energy of the teleportation spell vibrated in the quiet night, illuminating the faces of Emil and Fionna as they welcomed their friends.

Jasmin's eyes widened as they came into focus. "We did it. Wow, I wasn't completely sure we could make that jump."

Torie let out a deep breath. "Never a doubt in my mind." She laughed at the look Jasmin shot her. "Okay, mostly no doubts."

Max was bent over, hands on his knees. "That was... intense."

Jasmin slapped a hand on his back as she walked over to

Emil. "We made it though, didn't we?" Much to Emil's surprise, she reached out and pulled him into a tight hug. "Thank you, Emil."

The sprite blushed, the tops of his ears turning bright crimson. "I didn't really do anything. I mean, it was your idea that I keep this on me." He fished in his pocket and pulled out the black tourmaline gem. He held it out in the palm of his hand, offering it to the witch. Jasmin placed her hand around his and forced his fist closed around the stone.

"You keep it," she said. "The grounding properties it contains was what allowed us to focus on you and where you are. That allowed us to home in on this spot. On you."

Again, the sprite blushed. "Well, so see, it wasn't really anything I did. I just held onto a stone."

"Oh, you did more than that," said Torie, softly. "You filled that stone with your desire and your love. Don't think I didn't feel that." She turned away before his blush could threaten to overtake him. "I got your text. Were you able to find out what the convergence means?"

The sprite drew a deep breath and raised his shoulders while displaying the palms of both hands. "Perhaps. It's all very hard to interpret, you know."

"Just give us whatever you have," said Jasmin. "Anything will put us ahead of where we are now."

Emil nodded and scurried off to an area overgrown with tall grass and weeds, before returning, carrying a three-feet-long, stick shaped like a Y "Well, I have been experimenting with elemental dowsing, using it to detect energies and mystical patterns. We sprites have always been connected to the earth...maybe not in the same way as witches, but connected, nonetheless. However, unlike witches, we can't manipulate the forces we are attuned to. Still, it's always been a passion of mine. And when I arrived in Singing Falls, I knew the ley lines here were especially powerful. Moreso than any other place I have ever visited." While speaking, he had been focused on the dowsing rod in his hands, and when his eyes drifted up to those around him, he could see the slight frustration forming in their features. "Oh, yes...what does all that mean? Well, another thing we sprites are known for is our record keeping. What one sprite discovers, they record in a central library, so that it can then be known by all."

He motioned for them to follow him. He held the stick by the two branched ends, so that the single end protruded out in front of him. To the witches' surprise, the stick began to vibrate and swung itself in the direction of the large stone monolith that marked the entrance to Emberwood Hollow.

"This rod is made from Whisperwillow bark, a particularly potent mystical tree," Emil said, struggling to keep his grip on the dowsing rod that seemed determined to free itself from him.

Jasmin frowned. "I've never heard of this tree."

"Most aren't aware of it. It grows deep in the forest. In areas not traversed by humans. There's such an area farther up the mountain, you know. I'd be happy to take you one day."

Jasmin's eyes lit up. "I would very much love to see that."

Torie cleared her throat, bringing the two of them back to the matter at hand.

"Ah, yes...of course," said Emil, his attention returning to the dowsing rod. "In our records, I found tales of previous harmonic convergences and the impact they had on the supernaturals around them. These convergence records date back over the course of a few thousand years.

And each convergence resonates a specific magical frequency. And that frequency can tell us what the convergence's effect will be."

Torie's eyes widened. "Are you saying that you can predict what this convergence will be?"

"Well, to a degree, yes. I mean, nothing is perfect. We just need to know the frequency this convergence will resonate at."

Both witches stared at the sprite, until finally Jasmin spoke up. "So, can you tell us what it will be?"

Emil shook his head. "Oh, I have no idea how that works. The dowsing rod will find the nexus of the occurrence – and it appears to have already done so – but as for the color of the frequency…that requires a magic I do not have." He gave the two witches a piercing look.

Torie looked at Jasmin, her eyes hard and determined. "Okay, we can do this." She looked down at her watch. "And it looks like we are only going to get one shot at it. It will be midnight soon." She turned her attention back to Emil. "Where are the Umbrali?"

"They are gathered in the clearing inside the village," he said. "Rowena and Malena are there with them."

Torie nodded. "They'll be starting their ritual soon. Timing it to hit just before midnight I'm betting. Just before magic goes dark."

"Then we better make this fast," said Jasmin. "Emil, show us the nexus spot for the convergence."

The sprite released his grip on the dowsing rod, letting it zip through the air like a thing possessed, until it finally came to rest with the pointed end stuck in the ground directly in front of the monolith that heralded the entrance into Emberwood Hollow. There, buried halfway into the ground, it vibrated like a tuning fork that had just been struck.

Jasmin turned to Max and Elric. "You guys go find Fionna and keep an eye on what the Umbrali are doing. But don't engage. Hopefully we will join you soon with some information about what is going to happen."

The wolves agreed, with Elric planting a quick kiss on Torie and a squeeze of her hand, before they disappeared silently into the undergrowth. Once they were gone, the two witches turned their attention to the dowsing rod. Reaching out, they joined hands and magics, before speaking aloud.

> *"Rod of the Whisperwillow, may your truth reveal,*
> *tap into the power of the cosmic wheel.*
> *Harmonic convergence, event so rare,*
> *Show us the color that lingers there.*
> *By the ancient rites, by the olden lore,*
> *open the pathway, unlock the door.*
> *By the power of the stars, moon, and sun,*
> *reveal the hue of the convergence yet to come."*

The air sparkled around them as rainbow light grew in a bubble between them and the dowsing rod. Touched by magic, the rod began to vibrate even harder, until the Y portion of the stick was little more than a blur. Slowly, the rainbow light coalesced around it, settling between the points in a spinning ball. As it began to slow its rotation, it flashed through a kaleidoscope of colors until settling on a bright, calming blue.

Jasmin turned quickly to Emil. "Blue, what does that mean?"

The doctor already had his phone out, his round spectacles in place as he studied the screen.

"A cell phone?" asked Jasmin.

He quickly looked up at her. "We might come from an ancient race, but we are early adopters of all technology. How do you think we are able to upload and share our knowledge so quickly?" And with that, his head bent back to the device in his hand. He looked up with a smile, whipping off his glasses. "Blue is an excellent sign! Blue is the color of enhancement…but only for shifters, not witches."

"What does that mean for Elric, Max and the others?" asked Torie.

"It would explain why they have been acting so oddly the past couple of weeks leading up to tonight. Instead of their nature being suppressed by the convergence, it is being enhanced. They are becoming…more of what they are meant to be. Stronger, faster…maybe a bit more savage. But there is a chance they may not retain who they are as a person throughout the event. The human could be lost forever with only the animal remaining. It's very fascinating."

Torie's mind was spinning as she considered how best to utilize this new knowledge. Then a thought struck her. "And what does blue mean for witches?"

Emil frowned, wringing his hands together. "There is only one reference to be found regarding that. And all it states is…invergence."

"But no mention of our magic completely disappearing?" asked Jasmin.

"None that were recorded," replied Emil. "However, without knowing exactly what invergence refers to, I would caution against using your spells."

"Somehow, I don't think we are going to have much of a say in that," said Torie. She closed her eyes and her lips moved in a silent whisper. "I just told Elric what we learned and that under no circumstances should they shift. I just hope our rapport is still intact enough that he received it."

Jasmin nodded. "Okay. Time to go confront our brothers."

Torie's countenance was grim. "And put an end to this once and for all."

Chapter Twenty-Four

They made their way around the thickets to find Elric and Max. The wolves were crouched in the darkness with Fionna and Glen, their eyes trained on the clearing in front of the village houses. Gathered in the center of the clearing, a half-dozen characters stood, dressed in hooded robes identical to the ones worn by the hedge witches at the mansion.

But unlike the hedge witches, these men were not simple distractions. They radiated power.

They were standing before a large bonfire, roaring with life even though there was no perceived source of fuel for the flames. To the right of the figures, barely caught in the glow of the flickering flames, they could make out Rowena and Malena. The former stood still as a statue, still locked in place and held fast by powerful magics.

One of the figures stepped forward and raised his hand, pushing it into the fire. The flames turned from orange-yellow to emerald green. The figure stepped back and nodded to his companions as they stepped closer to the inferno and linked hands.

"Torie, do you feel that? The amount of magic they are giving off is insane," whispered Jasmin.

"Yeah. They are definitely ramping up for a major spell. We need to get down there," Torie said.

"Not alone you're not," said Elric, his voice low and steady.

"Elric, I told you not to shift…no matter what."

Max nodded to Fionna and Glen. "No one said we would."

Torie's attention was drawn to his hand where he held his police issued revolver. She turned to Fionna and Glen as they reached into a duffle bag at Glen's feet and withdrew matching shotguns. Her eyes widened as Elric reached into the bag and took out a particularly nasty-looking rifle equipped with a scope.

"Lecture us later," Elric said. "After we've stopped this."

Torie opened her mouth to protest, but Jasmin stopped her. "We don't have time to argue, Torie." She nodded in the direction of the Umbrali. They had created a semicircle, facing the flames, and now the chanting began.

> *"From the shadows of the void, beyond the veil,*
> *Hear our call, let the boundaries fail.*
> *In the abyss where no lights dwell,*
> *from silence below the depths of hell,*
> *awake, arise, heed our plea,*
> *cross the threshold, and to our world flee.*
> *We, the gatekeepers, do now invoke,*
> *break your chains, throw off your yoke.*
> *By the abyss, by the dark divine,*
> *we entreat thee now to cross the line.*
> *From your prison, to our land,*
> *on our summons, here you stand."*

The emerald fire bloomed before them, the flames dancing apart only to stretch and bend towards one another to form a large circle standing before the witches.

Torie looked at her watch. Minutes to go before midnight. "Come on. We need to stop this, now."

Together, the band of friends broke from the shadows, making their way towards the Umbrali.

"That's enough, magus," Torie shouted. She held her hands before her, orange globes of magic shimmered around them. Jasmin followed suit, adding her green glow to Torie's magic. The clicking sound of guns being cocked were the only other sounds in the forested area.

The cloaked figure that seemed to be the lead turned to them, raising his hands to push his hood back. There, beaming at the group of friends was a man in his early thirties, pleasant features and green eyes that peered out at them from beneath a mop of curly blond hair. While they hadn't been sure who they would be facing, the visage that now smiled at the friends was not it.

The leader nodded to his fellow Umbrali members, and they also removed their cloaks. All of the men before them ranged in age from late twenties to early forties at the oldest. They were all stylishly coiffed and well-manicured in their appearance. They all stared at the witches and their friends; the tips of their mouths turned upward in the same, unnerving grin.

"Well, hello there, sisters. I was beginning to think the hedge coven had proven to be too much for the two of you. I'm glad they weren't, however, because it's about time we got to meet in person. While I do go by a couple of different names, you can call me Charley. I'm the magus of the Umbrali." He leveled his gaze on Torie. "And you, are Torie." He then swung his head in Jasmin's direction.

"That would make you, Jasmin. It's an honor to meet you."

Jasmin scoffed at the man. "Hardly an honor.

Torie slowly advanced on the magus. "Charley, or whatever your name is, make no mistake. We came here to talk you out of whatever it is you're trying to do, but we are also prepared to use force to end this if we need to." She prayed the man could not see the beads of sweat starting to run down her forehead. She resisted the urge to look down at her watch. Surely it was past midnight already.

The magus looked from her to her friends, noting the tips of all their guns were trained solely on him.

"That's right," said Max. "We might not be able to take out all of your goon squad, but I guarantee you'll be the first to go if this goes sideways."

The magus raised his eyebrows. "You're going to kill me? With those primitive weapons? Even if I let you, I doubt those bullets would do me much harm. But why tempt fate?" With a quick flick of his wrist, the emerald ring of fire behind him flared, sending licks of light striking at the guns. In a flash, the weapons were vaporized.

All but one.

Torie felt her heart stop when her eyes fell on Elric. The wolf's arms were shaking, and his eyes were wide as they stared down the barrel of the rifle he had been carrying. The gun had torn itself from his grasp and now floated at eye level, inches from the wolf's forehead.

"No! Don't!" shouted Torie.

The magus sneered at her, his visage turning sour. "What happens next is one hundred percent on you. My coven will cut him down if you so much as breathe a spell in my direction. I'm going to need you and Jasmin to drop your magic." He reached into the folds of his robe and withdrew two sets of silver handcuffs. "And slip these on." He tossed them to the ground in front of the witches.

"Yeah, not happening. I know magic dampeners when I see them," said Jasmin.

Torie scanned the robed figures around him. They were focused on Elric, their lips moving as they silently invoked the magic holding the rifle in place.

She swallowed hard, her mind racing. Her hands were still raised, her magic encircling them. To her shock, her power flared briefly, the hum flickering and dying down before surging back to full strength.

"Interesting," said Charley. "Looks like the convergence is about to begin. Not much time for you to slip on your special jewelry there." He looked over his shoulder. The witches followed his gaze to see the center of the flaming circle had grown dark and murky. Smoke swirled, and they could clearly make out something moving behind the shadowy partition.

"Why are you doing this?" asked Torie as she bent to retrieve the handcuffs.

Charley smiled as she slowly slipped them on. "Now that's better. And as for why, that's simple. We are reclaiming our birthright." He lost the eerie smile with the last bit, as a snarl slipped free. "The power of the hex was ours to begin with. And then you women had to come along, taking and taking and taking. Tying the magic to your birthright." He spat the last word contemptuously. "For years, men with the right knowledge could train and tap into this magic. But you...all you had to do was be born into the right house. It's disgusting."

Jasmin laughed, drawing his attention. "So, all this is about your fragile male ego? You see someone else getting a taste of something you feel entitled to, and because of that you're going to what? Feed us to some beast from another realm?"

Now it was Charley who laughed. "No. Not at all. I don't want anything happening to you." His finger shot out, stabbing in Rowena's direction. "*She* is the gift to them. She will be the perfect sacrifice. Afterall, she was the one who gave our power to you women in the first place, all those thousands of years ago."

Jasmin rolled her eyes and turned to Torie. "Now ain't this some mess? This man complaining about something that happened millennia ago – literally – that probably had nothing to do with him...and yet he's mad about it." She narrowed her eyes and scanned the cloaked assemblage. "How old are you...children? See, Torie, you once asked me why we hex witches have to wait until we are forty to receive our powers. Well...because this is what happens otherwise."

Charley's face grew tight. "Put the silver on."

"Why? If you're so powerful, what potential threat can we hold over you?" Her eyes flashed as comprehension flowed across her features. "You're not the ones worried about us, huh? It's whatever that thing is that still hasn't set foot through your portal." She glanced down at her watch. "It's well after midnight and I can still feel my magic. So that means the convergence hasn't started yet. That means, what you're afraid of, is we can still stop this."

"Enough," Charley roared, nodding to his colleagues. "Play time is over." He looked at the gun floating in front of Elric's face. "Time to show you we mean business."

What happened next was faster than Torie could follow. All she heard was herself screaming just as Jasmin's magic flared around them. At the same time, there was the deafening crack of the rifle going off point blank at Elric's head.

189

Chapter Twenty-Five

Even through her ringing ears, Torie could hear her own scream. It burned at her soul, tearing her heart from her chest. She dropped to her knees, her vision clouding over as Elric dropped to the ground in a mist of red.

The numbness she felt was unlike anything she had ever known. In that moment, she ceased to breathe, to think…to exist. Everything she had hoped for in the future, everything that gave meaning to her, was now lying dead on the ground across from her.

And that was when she heard a growl. Low and deep, it reverberated across the grounds, rattling at the bones in her chest. She looked up, vision blurred through a waterfall of teardrops, and she saw something that made her question her sanity.

The growl was coming from Elric.

He was dragging himself up from the ground, pulling himself onto all fours, his head hanging low. Slowly, he raised it to reveal that while one cheek, an ear and an eye had been struck by the bullet, the massacred part of his face was quickly rearranging to that of a massive wolf. His body twisted, growing dark fur over bunched muscles the likes of which Torie had never seen.

Around his head, a mane of fur had formed, and three-inch fangs gleamed in the night. Torie looked down at massive paws sporting razor-sharp claws that he used to gouge at the earth. By one impossibly large paw something else caught her eye.

It was his silver bracelet that she had charmed to contain his wolf. It fizzled with the fading glow of emerald magic.

Jasmin's magic.

At the last minute, she had ripped it off Elric, freeing his werewolf. And that was the only thing that saved him from certain death.

Torie was mesmerized by the magnificent wolf that stood before them, a creature of such majestic scale that it dwarfed Elric's previous form. Its eyes, twin pools of molten gold, were luminous beneath the midnight hue of its fur. They simmered with an unspoken loathing as they fixed on the Umbrali. The thick sinews in his neck strained as he tilted his head towards the sky and unleashed an unearthly howl.

The sound was nothing less than an ethereal symphony. A haunting melody that poured from the depths of his soul. It cleaved through the silence, crystalline and piercing, as it resonated across the Hollow. It was a ballad wrought from the essence of the wolf, a primal chorus that echoed through the ages, reverberating with longing, love, and the unyielding will to protect.

The siren call died down and the world around them seemed to stop.

And then he charged.

The earth split under the power of his charge. As he rushed past Torie, a single, efficient swipe of his paws broke her handcuffs, leaving her skin miraculously unscathed. As he continued his charge at the Umbrali, Torie spun and threw her own magic at the magus. Her reaction was primal, and she reached for the part of her power that had always come the easiest to her.

Fire.

Only it wasn't. What should have been a ball of incendiary heat came out as a blast of polar air. Torie looked down at her hands in shock. The normal orange halo of magic that she was accustomed to was gone, replaced with a shimmer of pale blue and white. How was this possible? How could fire become ice?

Her eyes widened with understanding as she heard Emil's words repeated in her head. She looked over to Jasmin and shouted. "Invergence! Our magic has inverted."

Jasmin was already in the process of using her power as she reached deep into the soil, feeling for the vines and vegetation growing there, intending to send the roots forward to snatch up members of the Umbrali. The normal green signature of her power had turned a sickish gray with threads of black running through. The earth groaned before her, and she could feel the devastation her magic was causing. Instead of the vegetation growing and thriving under her touch, it retreated…fading and dying everywhere her magic touched. Immediately she stopped, staring at her hands incredulously.

"Well," said Charley. "Isn't this interesting?" He turned his attention from the witches to Elric who had advanced on the members of his clan. Taking a deep breath, his hand shot out at the flaming portal, and in return, the dark nimbus of swirling blackness at its center erupted out, spilling forth creatures from a dimension that had never seen sunlight.

Black and twisted, standing on bowed legs with arms that reached nearly to the ground, ending in claws or hooks rather than hands. Slobbering jowls filled with shark-like rows of teeth were open and gnashing as they advanced on Elric.

"Aw, the servants have arrived," Charley said, looking at a hapless Torie and Jasmin. "Soon, their master will step through and, in exchange for the earth goddess, it will grant us complete control over the ley lines on this plane. And when that happens, we will rewrite the laws of magic." He glared at the witches. "And the first of the new laws will be that women are forever cut off from the hex. Starting with the two of you." He spun around and waved his arm in Malena's direction. "And now, you can sit there helplessly and watch a daughter sacrifice her mother at the altar of power."

Torie stared impotently as Malena marched forward, the earth goddess gliding along behind her like a frozen sculpture being slid across an ice rink. Torie turned to face Charley, anger gathering in her as she saw the glee on his face. His eyes sparkling with insanity and magic.

Magic?

She turned to Jasmin. "They're still using magic! Either the convergence isn't affecting them, or..."

"They're not truly hex," finished Jasmin. "But something else. That or they are tapping into a source of magic- of hex power- that we haven't yet discovered."

Torie turned to see the creatures that had come through the portal circling Elric. The wolf roared in response, tearing at the earth and snapping his massive jaws as they closed in on him.

Torie looked at her hands again, afraid to even whisper a spell. Looking up, she could see the same worry flooding Jasmin. Before either could make a move, they heard a lone voice shout out.

"No! We will not be victims here!"

They turned to see Fionna screaming at the Umbrali. Rage poured from her as she sought out Malena. "I have been poisoned, hospitalized and seen my loved ones terrorized by you monsters. Well, no more!"

Torie watched as Fionna ripped away the piece of silver jewelry she wore. A bright flash of broken magic bloomed outward from the squirrel shifter as her body began to change. Her limbs twisted painful as they lengthened, fur sprouting from every inch of her, until she stood before them in a hybrid form. Her arms were long and muscular, her thighs had become cords of taut sinew. Her face elongated as whiskers protruded from a snout, with two gleaming white incisors showing from between her lips. Her body was covered in short, golden-hued fur that bristled with each breath she took. She drew herself up to a full six and a half feet and with a scream, leapt forward in long, powerful strides that carried her towards Malena and her captive.

As she finished transforming, Max did the same, removing the bracelet that bound his wolf.

Skin became fur, nails turned to claws and teeth to fangs in a glorious flash of spoiled magic. The very air around him trembled as he stepped free of his human form. Torie and Jasmin gasped audibly at the beast they now faced. It was a vision of terror and majesty made flesh. An alpha supernatural meant to rule at the top of a very violent food chain. With a roar that split the heavens, he covered the distance that separated him from Elric in a single bound.

Standing beside his now smaller beta, the wolves growled at the creatures from the portal.

And then they ripped into them.

Laughter echoed throughout the clearing as the magus filled the space with hateful glee. "It doesn't matter what your friends do. Once our new master makes his way into this world, the power of the ley is ours. And I will watch as you grovel powerless before us." His joy turned sour as he saw Fionna bounding across the open space, bearing down on Malena.

"No," he shouted, raising his hand to throw a blast of magic at the shifter. It struck her in the side, sending her careening off her feet and into the grove stand that bordered the clearing.

Taking advantage of the distraction, Malena doubled her efforts, heading towards the portal, Rowena in tow.

Shifting her attention to the portal, Torie saw the cloud of shadows reforming, this time they appeared to be throbbing in time with a rhythm she was thankful she couldn't feel. Something was preparing to come through.

Something big.

"What do we do?" she said to Jasmin. "We can try freeing Rowena…"

"But we could just as easily destroy her. Our magic is basically useless until the convergence is over."

"And by that time, we probably won't have our powers anymore."

They turned to focus on the melee that was happening between Elric and Max and the horde of creatures they were fighting. Despite their new food size and strength, they were barely holding their own against monsters that seemed to keep pouring forth from the portal. The wolves would destroy two creatures, and four more would take their place.

It was only a matter of time before Max and Elric fell. Even at the peak of their abilities, there was only so much they could do.

There was a thud behind them, and the witches turned to see two of the shadow creatures standing a few feet away. They were hunched over, clawed hands dragging the ground, a vile, yellowish mucous dripping from their slavering jaws.

They reached for the witches, their large, blank eyes locking on the two friends. And then the undergrowth rattled, and a blur bounded forth.

Fionna was on the two creatures before they knew what hit them. She struck the first across the face, her powerful claws tearing away half of its skull. The second moved faster in reaction to the assault, but compared to Fionna it might as well have been mired in tar. It turned, reaching for the shifter, only to have Fionna grasp its arm and wrench it free. Then, she vaulted over the top of the beast, one hand snagging it under the chin on the way down. She landed, pulling the beast's head backwards until a sickening crunch left it lying in a heap on the ground.

Fionna stood, staring down at the witches, her eyes feral, as she rocked back and forth. Then, she looked up, her nose quivering as she scented the air.

"Go," she said in a voice that was raw and gravely. And before either Torie or Jasmin could respond, she was gone, bounding in the direction of the portal.

Jasmin gasped, then cried out for her to stop. But it fell on deaf ears as the squirrel shifter, their best friend, dove headfirst into the portal.

Chapter Twenty-Six

"Fionna!" The scream tore from Glen, audible even over the din of teeth gnashing bones, and the roar of wolves. Without hesitation, she ran to the spot where her gun had been thrown once it was ripped from her hands. The boom from her shotgun rang out across the clearing as she moved forward, firing shot after shot at the creatures around her.

"They're barely feeling those shots," said Jasmin. "We have to do something."

Before they could act, Torie watched in horror as one of the creatures spun on Glen, sweeping aside the shotgun and scooping her up in a clawed fist. The woman screamed, but not in agony. She screamed out in anger and defiance.

Torie closed her eyes and breathed a silent plea for strength as she raised her hands to unleash magic over which she no longer had control. Jasmin's hand on her shoulder stopped her.

"Do you feel that?" Jasmin asked.

There was a rumble through the ground. Torie could feel it through her boots. It was slight but growing fast. So fast that in a fraction of a second, it felt like she was standing on the tracks of an approaching freight train.

And that was when the darkness around them erupted as a multitude of shapes burst from the tree line, stampeding towards the clearing. Some of the shapes ran on two legs, but the majority were on all fours, eating up the ground at a remarkable speed. The creatures from the portal turned to face the incoming wall, and the cloaked Umbrali gathered, hands raised, ready to defend themselves, the magus, and protect Malena and Rowena.

"The shifters from Emberwood Hollow," said Jasmin. "They've all come back to help. But how…?"

Torie nodded. "Elric. That howl he gave was more than just a howl."

"It was a call to arms," whispered Jasmin.

The witches watched as the tidal wave of shifters, each possessing the ultimate evolution of their form, crashed forward into the creatures. Torie breathed a sigh of relief as she saw a bear shifter carefully pick up Glen and toss her onto its back. Then, picking up Glen's shotgun and slinging it back to her, they rode into battle together, blasting and clawing at anyone that stood before them.

"The tide is turning," said Jasmin.

"But for how long?" Torie's eyes were locked on the portal. Malena had made her way to it with Rowena and the magus standing next to her. Their window to act was slowly beginning to close, and she knew it. "We have to get down there. Who knows what could be happening to Fionna right now?"

A rustling behind them caught their attention. Emil stepped forward to greet them, his hair disheveled and his face smudged with dirt. "They have had years to plan this out. You can't fight them on their terms. They were prepared for the invergence. Remember, your magic is not gone; it's just new to you. Again." He stepped backwards, blending into the dark foliage. "Do what you do best."

The two witches looked at one another, faces stern and resolute. They joined hands and walked across the clearing towards where Malena and Rowena stood alongside the magus.

From Jasmin's side, a creature with red dripping from its jowls leapt at them, claws extended. The witch reached out with her hand, made a fist and pulled it back sharply towards her. The beast, gripped by an invisible force, found itself flung backwards and away from Jasmin with such force that it stormed into another of its kind with back-breaking force.

From Torie's side, two of the cloaked Umbrali approached, arms raised as they began to chant. Torie's eyes flashed as she reached out with her magic. She called on her fire and, as expected, ice structures flowed up and around the men, encasing them in large shards of ice.

Torie looked at Jasmin. "Maybe this isn't so bad."

"Parlor tricks." They turned to see Malena addressing them. "They won't work against the magus, and they certainly will have no effect on the master when he comes through."

"Get out of the way, Malena," Jasmin said, her voice low and hard. "Our friend is in there and we are getting her out. So, we don't have time to play with you."

Malena's face grew deep red at Jasmin's words. "Again, you treat me as if I am nothing. I am sick of constantly being dismissed." She held out her hand and a particularly nasty knife appeared in her palm. It was silver, with a curved blade. She leaned close and whispered to it, causing red sigils to appear emblazoned on the blade. With a smile, she held it to Rowena's throat. "You think I won't do it?"

"I know you will," said Torie. "You've shown us who you are. But I don't think your boss is going to like you doing that to his offering." She glanced to the side and saw that Charley was cautiously approaching her.

"Malena, stop," he said, his voice warm and filled with concern.

If Torie hadn't known better, she would have thought he genuinely cared for her. And that gave her an idea. "Malena, you're saying we don't care, that we are dismissive and only want to control you. Well, what do you think *he* wants?"

The young woman stared at her, eyes slowly narrowing. "Stop it. You're just trying to get in my head. Just like before."

Torie shook her head. "That isn't true. We were always truthful and upfront with you. Can he say the same?" She jutted her chin in Charley's direction.

The magus gave her one of his biggest grins yet, then leaned in close to Malena. "You know what they are doing, right? More distractions, more mind games. It's what they do. They want to confuse you."

"Lies," said Torie. "Malena, who has been manipulating who all this time? Who has repeatedly used you to get what they wanted?"

The girl frowned, the knife in her hand wavered slightly but remained pointed at Rowena's throat. Would she even be able to kill Rowena with that thing? It wasn't something Torie wanted to risk. The glowing glyphs on the blade told her the dagger was more than just ceremonial.

"Malena," said Jasmin, "what do you think they are going to do once that thing comes through the portal?

They've come right out and said how they feel about female magic practitioners."

"Your place at our table is secure, little one," said the magus. "You have proven your worth. You will be one of us, you know that."

Torie scoffed. "He didn't even address you by your name, Malena. He called you *little one*. In his mind, you're a child and therefore, will always be beneath him." She glanced at the portal. The shadows had built up again since Fionna had disappeared into the opening. Something was moving once more, stirring the murkiness.

Time was running out.

All around them the fight raged. Shifters growled, monsters raged, wolves howled, and Glen's shotgun boomed. Torie could feel Jasmin's agitation. They needed to get Fionna.

If she was still in there. If she was still alive.

"We are running out of time," Jasmin whispered.

Torie didn't take her eyes off the magus and Malena, but nodded just enough so that only Jasmin would notice. She also knew that at this point, they had a decision to make. Try to get into the portal to help Fionna or tackle the magus and potentially save Rowena. She was the key to this. Without her to offer up, the magus wouldn't be able to fulfill whatever deal he had with the monster on the other side of the veil.

That would translate to saving all of Singing Falls and beyond. She looked at Jasmin, her eyes conveying the dilemma. There really was no choice.

A disturbance behind the shadows of the portal caught everyone's attention. A moan escaped the circle, low in timbre, rolling across the space like a fetid summer wind carrying the promise of death and despair.

"It's time!" exclaimed the magus, his voice filled with reverence and expectation. He turned his delirious smile on Malena. "And you know what that means?" He leaned in close to the girl. "It means, you should have listened to the witches."

It happened fast. There was a flash, the sound of skin being pierced, the widened eyes of a woman who had been little more than the means to an end for too many people.

"No!" Torie shouted as the tip of a knife protruded through the center of the girl's chest before turning into a black vapor and disappearing.

Malena looked down, her eyes wide in shock and disbelief. She turned her face towards the magus, her mouth forming a small O that no words escaped. Then, slowly, she crumpled to the ground, still staring silently up at the man in which she had placed the last bit of her trust.

"Oh well, that wasn't supposed to happen this quickly," said the magus with a shrug, "but you two made me up the timeline on it a bit." He looked past the witches and smiled at the portal. "I think it's time."

Thunder rolled overhead, even though no lightning was present. The magus looked around, the tiniest of frowns creasing his features as he glanced to the heavens. He looked around at the chaos still erupting as fighting carried on and signaled to his fellow Umbrali. "It's time, brothers. Gather around and prepare to receive your gifts on this wondrous night."

The Umbrali who were still standing retreated, standing next to the magus and Rowena. Their hands were raised, ready to deflect any of the shifters that might try charging through the line of dark creatures that fought to hold everyone else at bay. Only the Umbrali leader, his followers, and Torie and Jasmin were going to be allowed to witness the entrance of whatever evil the cabal had struck a deal with.

Again, the thunder rolled overhead, this time booming louder, causing the trees surrounding the clearance to shake with the reverberations. The air around them grew oppressively hot, making it difficult to draw breath.

"What in the world is all this?" asked Jasmin.

"It is the arrival of true glory," said the magus, looking at the portal with reverence.

"Somehow, I don't think so," said Torie, giving Jasmin a nudge.

They looked at Rowena, still frozen in place, the shards of the crystal bottle still glinting as they protruded from her skin and clothing. Only something was different.

It was her eyes.

They were lifeless and unblinking as before, but there was something behind them. Something black that seemed to be rolling with the thunder. Something that beat in time with the rhythmic, staccato bursts.

Taking a quick glance at the increased activity in the portal, the witches knew that it was then or never for them to strike. They joined hands, reaching for the magic that had always come so easily to them. The security they felt with their power wasn't there; something foreign and scary had replaced it.

Something that shrank away from them when they tried to touch it.

As the rumble overhead increased, they closed their eyes, syncing what magic they could, and began to chant.

"Bound in glass, under lock and key,
remain concealed for all eternity.
With chains of ice, your power we quell,

in this icy prison, may you always dwell.
Elements align, heed our call,
strengthen her chains, let not them fall.
By power of frost, by power of stone,
we command that you remain forever alone.
In the heart of ice, where no warmth lies,
let the earth goddess close her eyes.
May her strength be trapped, her spirit bound,
in darkness' embrace, never to be found."

Magic flared, dark as ink, the earth roiled, heaving in defiance of the witches' touch. And then, a burst of lightning split the sky, streaking earthward in a blinding strike.

And when everyone's vision cleared from the flash, they focused on Rowena. The earth goddess was freed, her flesh seared by the heat of the lightning bolt. She leveled her vision on the magus, eyes flashing, and raised her hand in his direction.

Chapter Twenty-Seven

"No, wait," Torie said, stepping between Rowena and the magus, spreading her arms to shield the Umbrali leader.

Rowena's eyes never left the man as she addressed Torie. "Step away. You have done enough this day in setting me free. This...man, has killed one whom I breathed life into. He has orchestrated the impossible by imprisoning me. I intend to see that he does not witness another sunrise in this life."

"And you have every right to do that," she replied, glancing at Malena's body. "But if you do, you make him a martyr to many who will see what he did as a challenge and an opening. Do you think he will be the last of his kind to attempt this?"

The earth goddess didn't speak, only continued to stare at the magus, her eyes glowing brilliantly in the night.

The magus laughed harshly at the women. "Go ahead. Do it. We were the first to wield the power. We were the first to track the harmonic convergence and pass that knowledge down, waiting for the one that would benefit us and allow us to open the black portal. We made the deal with that other-worldly master…we showed it where to find a land ripe with ley lines that can be tapped to create new dynasties in this world and others. Do you think the master is just going to forget? Five hundred years is the blink of an eye to one such as they…you'll all be dust and it will still be eager to consume this plane of existence."

Jasmin shook her head. "He's right. What he's done here will have a ripple effect. All we can do is prepare the following generation for –" Her words were cut off sharply as dark clouds billowed forth from the portal.

"Stand behind me," said Rowena. "I will deal with this monstrosity." Thunder boomed again; this time preceded by flashes of intense lightning as Rowena readied herself to face what was to come.

The members of the Umbrali shrank away from the portal as all eyes were focused on the fiery circle.

The magus dropped to his knees, raising his face and hands towards the heavens. "Yes. Yes! It is time." He turned to face the witches, gloating. "You're all about to die."

Torie's eyes widened. "Rowena…close the portal!"

But before the earth goddess could act, the portal expanded as something began to push its way through. The shadows clung to the figure like thick smoke, obscuring the creature's details. but slowly, those assembled could make out large, twisted horns, black in color, dripping with a dark and viscous substance. The horns parted the dark curtain and soon the witches saw they were attached to a forehead that was ashen, with an array of smaller horns just breaking through.

The face appeared next, jagged and pointed, massive in size, with lips pulled back from a row of curved, pointed teeth. The tongue was hanging out, lolling to one side as more of the creature's face appeared. Eyes that were sunken sat atop a pointed nose that lay flush against the skull.

But as they looked closer, Torie and Jasmin realized something was wrong with the eyes. They were dull and lifeless, protruding and unseeing.

"Rowena, don't!" Torie shouted at the last minute.

What appeared next took everyone's breath away. The creature's massive head pushed itself the rest of the way through the portal, only there was no body with it. Instead, it was held aloft, facing the assemblage, gripped fiercely by a clawed hand.

Torie nearly burst into tears as Fionna stepped through the portal, holding her grisly trophy which she unceremoniously tossed to the ground, letting it roll forward a few feet to come to rest facing the Magus, who could only stare in disbelief.

Fionna stood there, breathing hard, covered in a mixture of blood and the same viscous substance that covered the creature's horns. One of her arms was turned at an awkward angle and of the many gashes on her body, there was an oblique slice across her torso that looked especially bad. The squirrel shifter spat blood and let out a series of hacking coughs that hinted at internal injuries.

Her lithe muscles spasmed in pain as she struggled to hold herself upright. But she never wavered. Her eyes, tiny specs of darkness, glinted in her hybrid features as they darted about the group of supernaturals. The creatures that had been fighting the shifters had stopped all motion. Their attention flicked from the head of the beast that lay before them, to Fionna's fur and blood-covered body and neck, to the beast. Slowly, as realization began to set in, they shuffled away from the shifter clan and made their way back to the portal, back to whatever darkness from which they spawned.

The shifter ranks split, and Glen burst forward, throwing her arms around Fionna.

"I thought I had lost you," she whispered.

Fionna looked down at her through a swollen, black eye. "Unlike that thing, I don't die that easy." She tried to laugh but ended up racked in a spasm of coughing. Glen wound her arm around her wife's back and helped her to a wooden bench where Emil quickly appeared to assist her.

The magus stared at the head lying before him, his face twisting in emotions before he roared in anger. "How dare you? I am going to enjoy this." He leapt to his feet, raising one arm and sending a blast of black flames at Fionna.

Both Emil and Glen instinctively jumped in front of the shifter, shielding her body with their own. But the flames never reached them. Instead, they flickered and died out, midair, leaving the magus to stare at his hands.

"How…?" he murmured.

Rowena's voice rang out clear and strong. "Even as I was imprisoned, I wondered how you were able to continue to work your magic. Hex magic doesn't work under the auspices of the harmonic convergence." She gave Torie and Jasmin a quick smile. "At least not the way you were using it. So that told me you were tapping into something else. A wholly new source of power, from a place outside the touch of the convergence." Her eyes drifted to the severed head before them. "And now I know where that source originated. But with this monster dead, the power he granted you died as well. And until the convergence passes, you won't have full access to your hex magic." She turned to Torie and Jasmin. "How you managed to do what you did is impressive. I would not have thought of working reverse magic the way you did."

"How long until the convergence is over?" asked Jasmin,

looking over at the shifters. "And when it's over, will they all return to normal?"

Rowena nodded. "Not much longer and all will be as it was. At least for another five hundred years." She looked at the body of Malena, her smile fading, her eyes growing moist.

"I promise you; we will see that she is taken care of," said Torie.

"Don't worry. She will be going with me when I leave this place." Her gaze darkened and turned back to the magus. "And that brings me back to you." She walked over to the man as he cowered before the women. "You know, it was my power that enabled the tapping into the ley lines all those millennia ago. I am the source for both hedge and hex magic. What you sought from that demon…the dominion over the power in the earth, has always been mine to give. You had me trapped and could have taken from me what you wanted. Instead of making a deal with…that."

Torie's eyes lit up. "Wait, are you saying you are able to give someone the ability to use hex magic? Does that mean you can also take it away?"

Rowena gave her a curious look. Then all eyes fell to the magus.

"No," he said, his voice frail. "You can't. You wouldn't…"

"Do you know why the power of the hex flows so easily, so powerfully with these two?" Rowena said, gesturing towards Torie and Jasmin. "There's no secret formula. It isn't because they are women. It is because they are worthy. Magic will always flow to those who will respect and cherish it and use it to protect those around them. Yes, you can bully your way into it, but it will never truly belong to you. And the fact that it is something you want to solely possess? That speaks volumes about what it would be used for in your hands." She sighed, looking around. "The convergence is nearly over. Soon, your magic will return. But you are not worthy of those gifts."

Without a word, she quickly placed her palm on the man's head. He jumped; his body convulsed as if struck by lightning. He gasped, his eyes rolling briefly to the back of his head.

"What…what did you just do?" he managed.

"I have sealed you off from the source," she said. She waved her arm in an arc, and all of the Umbrali fell to their knees. "You and your cadre will never again know the touch of the hex."

"You will pay for this," the magus groaned.

Rowena looked at the small body lying on the ground. "I already have. Now, be thankful for your sisters, and remember this day. For this is the day you were given the gift of life." Her eyes grew cloudy, and her voice grew to rumble like thunder. "Because were it up to me, I would have ended your existence in a much more fitting fashion."

The magus was shaking his head in despair. "You should. You should have killed me. I'd rather be dead than live this way."

Rowena smiled and spoke in a cryptic tone. "You may yet get your wish…"

Torie and Jasmin looked at her, confused, before Torie turned to the portal. "Any issues with that?"

Rowena shook her head. "With the magic that fed it gone, it is already fading. You have nothing to fear. But there is something I would discuss with you. The two of you have my eternal gratitude. I saw the way you tried to help my wayward child. Her undoing was no fault of yours. But as a way of thanking you, I offer you a parting gift. Before the convergence ends, I can grant you something; whatever is within the power of the ley, I can give to you. Would you like your magical abilities increased? Longer lifespans? Power over the weather perhaps? Tell me quickly and it is yours."

Torie and Jasmin exchanged shocked looks. Mouths agape as they stood before the earth goddess. They smiled to one another, suddenly each knowing what they wanted.

Torie turned to her friends. "If it is within the power of the ley lines, I would like for all shifters to retain the ability to shift into their most evolved forms, with complete control over these abilities. They are brave, and kind, and without a doubt the best people I know." She looked at Fionna, her eyes moist. "Let them be what they are ultimately meant to be."

Elric rushed to her side, his eyes glowing brightly in his giant wolf form. When he spoke, his voice was deep and ragged. "Torie, no. You can't waste such a gift on us. We are not —"

"And so it shall be," said Rowena. She raised both hands, and the wind began to whip around her. Malena's body lifted off the ground held aloft by the gentle winds. "Farewell, witches of Singing Falls. Know that I am in your debt, now and forever." She gave one last look towards the broken magus. "And remember what you wished for, little man..."

And with that, she was gone, a single bolt of light that shot her and Malena towards the heavens. The wind died instantly, and the dark clouds parted, revealing a sky sparkling with countless points of light.

"What...what did she m-mean by that?" the magus muttered.

Looking around, Torie's face was grim. "I think it's time for us to leave."

She and Jasmin walked over to Fionna where they helped her stand. Accompanied by Elric, Max, Glen and Emil, they headed slowly into the clearing and away from the shifter village. None of them looked back as the shifters slowly corralled the Umbrali and advanced towards them, the lowest of rumbles echoing across the field.

The only sound that followed the friends out of the clearing was one short scream quickly choked out in the night air.

Chapter Twenty-Eight

Under the generous shade of a grand old red oak, Torie, Jasmin, Fionna and Glen lounged on Torie's expansive back deck. Even though battle fatigue still lingered, the day itself wrapped them in a warm blanket of comfort.

The sky above was a glorious canvas of Carolina blue marred only by the occasional cotton-candy cloud as it passed through. The mixture of earthy scents wafting from Torie's greenhouse, mixed with the smoky hardwoods drifting from the grill was heavenly. A serving tray holding a large pitcher of fresh sangria, with iced glasses, floated towards the four friends.

"Now this," Glen said, reaching for a glass, "is the life." They each took a glass and clinked them together in salutations before settling back into their teak recliners.

Jasmin looked over at the grill where Emil was animatedly giving Max directions on how and when to flip the steaks. She smiled to herself as it was obvious the big wolf was having nothing to do with being told how to grill. "Look at those two. To look at them you'd think they were polar opposites, but deep down they're a lot more alike than they're willing to admit."

They all laughed, taking sips and placing their drinks on the small tables near each seat.

Torie reached over and placed her hand over Fionna's. "You okay?"

The squirrel shifter nodded, reaching up to fiddle with the oversized sunglasses she wore. "I am. Or I will be. I'm just glad to be here with everyone." She squeezed Torie's hand and then reached to take her wife's. She still hadn't spoken about what had happened inside the portal, and Torie knew not to push it. She would open up when the time was right, and until then, the only thing she had to know was that she was loved and supported.

"I still can't believe how fast you healed," said Glen. "I mean, that was a compound break in your arm, and your liver was lacerated. Yet, here you are, not a mark on you."

"Well, you can thank Torie and Jasmin for that. Those injuries would have killed the old me, I'm pretty sure. But in that new, evolved, hybrid form...I felt like I could do anything. And as painful as it was shifting back to human, I could feel my human self beginning to mend almost right away. It was unreal."

Torie blushed. "I've never seen anything like the bravery you displayed, throwing yourself into that portal like that." She shuddered at the memory.

Fionna smiled. "Well, all I could think in the moment was, 'what would Torie do'?"

They all enjoyed a laugh at that. Torie sank back, letting the warmth of the sun rain down on her. In that moment, they weren't witches, or shifters, or warriors returning home from a victorious battle.

In that moment, they were just friends, enjoying each other's company.

"What are those two up to?" asked Jasmin, jutting her chin out in the direction of the pool house across from them.

Torie sat up and lowered her glasses, taking in Elric and Leo. The werewolf was sitting on the edge of the finally completed pool, his legs dangling in the crystal water. His hands were moving quickly as he spoke to the little dragon, who buzzed in front of him, flitting from one side of the wolf to the other, his scales flashing from one color to another in excitement.

"Who knows? Probably plotting what room full of furniture they're going to destroy next, all in the name of *play*," she said with a laugh.

Before she could lean back, the little dragon zipped across the water, wings buzzing furiously.

"Hey!" shouted Elric, hopping up and rushing around the pool to join them. "Don't!"

Torie sat up, then the women around her focused on the dragon as he hovered in midair.

"Yes! Yes! Yes!" he said, spinning in place.

"Leo, what are you going on about?" Torie said. She looked over and Emil and Max had also walked up, standing behind the dragon, just as Elric raced to his side.

"That is the last time I tell you anything," said Elric in a forced whisper to the little dragon.

There was silence around them that suddenly captured Torie's attention. She sat bolt upright, worry seeping into her bones.

Elric sighed, reaching up and scratching his head. Then, taking a deep breath, he dropped to one knee in front of the witch.

Torie gasped, her heart fluttering furiously. Beside her, Jasmin's hand flew to her mouth while Glen and Fionna sat perfectly still clasping tightly to one another.

Elric cleared his throat. "Torie, from the moment I first saw you, I knew there was something special about you. Your courage, your selflessness, your beauty. But most of all, it was your compassion and kindness. The way you care for everyone around you; it's more powerful than any spell you could cast."

His hand trembled as he reached into his pocket and pulled out a small, velvet box, cradling it as though it held the world's most precious treasure – because to him, it did. "You have walked with me through moonlit forests and stood by my side during the fiercest of battles. You've shared my joys, soothed my sorrows, and accepted me in all my forms."

He opened the box to reveal the most beautiful, delicate ring Torie had ever seen. Nestled atop a white gold band was a moonstone that shone with a delicate blue light. Arranged around it was an assortment of tiny diamonds, starlike in their beauty and clarity. "I am a shifter by nature, forever moving between two worlds. But one thing remains constant, my love for you. You have always given so much, and as selfish as it may seem, I am going to ask you for one more thing." He took a deep breath, his eyes shimmering as he held back tears. "Torie, will you marry me?"

It seemed like the world held its breath for an eternity before Torie reached out and pulled him to her. Tears streamed down her face as she enthusiastically bobbed her head up and down.

"Yes," was all she could manage before letting out a sob. "A thousand times, yes."

"Yes, yes, yes!" echoed Leo, flying in circles and blowing blue flame into the air.

They all laughed and raised glasses. Torie cried, Jasmin cried, Fionna cheered. And even though they all knew that somewhere out there, something dark and twisted was plotting something unthinkable, it could wait. Because right then, in that moment, everything in Singing Falls, was just perfect.

More by M.J. Caan

vinci-books.com/goodmagic

She didn't ask for magic. But fate's got other plans.

When Allie's attacked by the undead, her dormant powers awaken
—and so do ancient enemies. With a failing spell guarding
humanity and a dark legacy rising, she must master her magic
fast… or watch the world fall into darkness.

Turn the page for a free preview…

The Girl with the Good Magic:
Chapter One

Of all the myriad magical gifts my mother was purported to possess and could have passed on to me, precognition was not one of them. Yet moments before a dead, rotting thing attacked us, I had been working at my family's coffee shop, listening to my best friend drone on, and I had just thought to myself: *Once, just once, I'd love for something exciting to happen in this town.*

"Earth to Allie...you there?"

The snapping of fingers in my face brought me back to reality.

"Sorry," I said. "I was daydreaming."

"In the middle of my read? Wait, were you daydreaming about my future?" Hope said excitedly. She's my best friend and the look in her almond-shaped eyes was way too hopeful for this early on a Saturday morning.

"What? No. I'm sorry, where were we?"

Hope motioned to the sludge at the bottom of her coffee cop. "You were about to tell me that someone tall, dark and handsome is about to waltz into my life, sweep me up into their arms and take me out of this little hole-in-the-wall town. Preferably in a white Lamborghini."

I couldn't help but roll my eyes. "Like I'd let you be part of a Harlequin cliche."

"Well," she said, "what do you see? I mean, what's the point in having a psychic for a best friend if you can't tell me the good stuff before it happens to me?"

"I'm not a psychic, Hope. I've told you that."

"Psychic. Witch. Whatever," she said flippantly.

"Hope! What have I told you about saying things like that when we are in a public place?" I glanced up from behind the counter at the coffee shop to see if anyone noticed. Luckily, nobody had looked up from their laptop, and the fact that most of the patrons had earbuds in helped me to breathe easier as well.

Hope rolled her eyes dramatically at me. "No one pays attention to anything that happens in here. Besides, the tourists come in here for readings, so what's the big deal?"

Trinity Cove was a tourist's destination. Every summer what seemed like a million people came traipsing into our idyllic little town nestled in mountains of North Carolina. They come for the natural beauty of the region; lakes, hiking, quaint bed and breakfasts and access to some of the best furniture galleries in the country. But mostly they come to see the Singing Falls. An hour-plus, depending on the path you took, hike up some of the toughest trails in the region would take you to a secluded lagoon that was fed by a one-hundred-foot waterfall. The water poured down into the natural pool over jagged, protruding rock outcroppings that sheltered multiple caverns carved into a mountainside. Because the rock outcroppings that the water cascaded over were thin and their openings hollow, the sound of the water flowing down was haunting; the echoes created were of varying pitches and constantly changing due to climate and shifts in the topography they ran across.

It also made for treacherous footing along the sides of the fall. Every summer at least one person fell down the steep pitch, breaking legs, arms, and on a couple of occasions, necks.

Still, the undeniable scenic beauty called to people from all walks of life and they descended on the town in droves every year. Their money went a long way to keeping the town's coffers filled, and all of the sleepy businesses in Trinity Cover catered to them during the tourist season. Restaurants advertised the freshest homemade delicacies, even though they were the same meals that could be purchased year round at a much steeper discount. Signs popped up in numerous yards advertising antiques for sale. Every home with an extra bedroom was suddenly a bed and breakfast. Every semi-athletic college dropout that still lived at home with his or her parents was suddenly a canoe guide promising to take you to a secret spot upriver that only the locals know about.

Yeah. That kind of small town.

And I have to admit, I was just as much to blame as everyone else in the town. My Aunt owned the 3 Coves Cafe and Bakery that sat on a prime spot in the center of the town square. I was one of those college dropouts that had decided to live at home while I found myself. I ran the café, and one of my side gigs for summer was to act as the town fortune teller. Instead of tea leaves I would read coffee sludge.

My best friend Hope had just arrived home from her first year of college and had been regaling me with tales of drunken frat parties, all-night jam sessions followed by ditching the class you just stayed up all night studying for.

Oh, and the men. She was convinced that the state college she was attending was where she was going to meet Mr. Right and head off into the sunset with him.

Her badgering look snapped me out of my reverie and I gazed into the bottom of her ceramic cup.

"Nope," I said. "There's nobody in there. But hey, after one whole year away from home, what are you expecting?"

Hope bristled at my tone. It had come out a lot more terse than I intended.

"Well, at least I'm away from home and trying."

Ouch. Touché and all that.

"I'm sorry." Her tone instantly softened. "I didn't mean that the way it sounded." She reached across the counter and placed her hand on top of mine to give it a reassuring squeeze.

"No problem." I smiled. "I kind of deserved that one." I turn and placed her cup in the bin on the back table so it could be bussed into the kitchen and cleaned. Turning back, I smiled again. "But really, why are you in such a hurry to get hitched? You have your whole life ahead of you." I flinched a little. I already knew the answer to that question, but I wanted to see if she would confirm my thoughts.

"It's hard," she said, eyes downcast. "My mom wants to see me in the wedding gown she made for me so bad. I want her to see that as well." Hope's eyes clouded up and I could see her clenched her jaw to stave off tears.

"Hey." Now it was my turn to reach out and grab her hand. "The doctors don't know everything. She beat breast cancer once before and she can beat it this time around as well."

"Thanks for that," Hope said. "I feel like an ass even saying that, considering your mom is…"

"No worries. My mom bailed on Gar and me years ago.

He doesn't really remember her. He was too young when she left."

It was true. My brother Garland, or Gar as he preferred to be called, had long forgotten what our mother looked like. He could remember the stories she told us when he was small, but time had long since erased the mental imagery of her from his mind's eye.

Unfortunately, my mental imagery was as strong as ever. If I closed my eyes I could still picture our mother's face. Not just the green eyes and fire-red hair that I had inherited, but also the tiny curves around her full lips and the lines that danced around her eyes when she laughed. Our mother had been so happy when we knew her. But that was before the madness set in; before she began to whisper about demons and monsters that hid in the woods outside of the house we shared with Aunt Vivian and Aunt Lena.

At least, I had always hoped it was madness.

I came from a long line of witches. Not just any witches, but rock star witches if you believed what my mother had told us as children. According to her, she and my aunts stopped Armageddon from devouring our sleepy little town in the form of werewolves.

While Gar could remember the stories as only bedtime tales, I remembered them as something more: a cautionary tale of what had once nearly wiped out all of Trinity Cover, and could possibly happen again. To Gar, they were heroic and funny. But I was older; to me they were horrific and the cause of night terrors that occasionally would still wake me from fitful nights of sleep.

Our aunts had assured us that the stories our mother told us were just that: stories meant to entertain and frighten children who stayed up long past their bedtime.

While we may have been called witches at one time, my

aunts assured us that moniker was one that was never merited. We might have small gifts, the occasional extra-sensory ability, or a way with certain potions and herbs that did little more than induce euphoria in townsfolk and allowed them to sleep better, but that was it. We didn't fly around on broomsticks. We didn't cast spells.

And we certainly weren't responsible for the destruction of an entire breed of supernatural creatures referred to as werewolves.

The fact is, here in town my family had a certain repu-tation. We weren't shunned, but we weren't exactly asked over for Sunday dinners either. People here had a grudging respect for my aunts. They were polite to them, some were even friendly, but most stopped just short of crossing the street when they saw one of my aunts heading toward them on the same sidewalk.

They were a little suspicious when I told them I wanted to add fortune telling to the seasonal offerings at the coffee shop, but after they saw the bump in business, they allowed me my indulgences. I wasn't a clairvoyant in the true sense of the word. My medium abilities were mostly the product of being able to read a person's emotional state and combine it with the latest horoscope readings I found online. Add to that a few vague, generic missives from Google and voila...your very own fortune told.

Hope wasn't a tourist however, and she wouldn't fall for the mumbo-jumbo that I spewed to most of the giggling schoolgirls who passed through in the summer. No, she had been my best friend since grade school. She knew what I went through, she knew what the townies whispered about my family, and she knew when to call bullshit on me.

"C'mon, Allie," she pleaded. "I know when you're lying. You saw something. Spill it!"

The truth was I hadn't seen anything, and that was why my gaze had lingered in the cup. Usually there was something; a small spark, or flash of something brief and tiny that revealed itself to me. I may or may not opt to tell the person, but there was almost always something there. That was especially true with the people I was close to. But this time, when I looked into the coffee grinds all I saw was... coffee. I felt numb and cut off from the tiny spark of my vision.

No. Not cut off. Blocked. I opened my mouth to tell Hope that I really didn't see anything, but my words were cut off by the sudden wail of a siren followed by the revving of a car engine as a police cruiser tore down main street, lights and siren blaring. It was quickly followed by the similar sounds of an ambulance as it chased after the cruiser.

"What the..." exclaimed Hope, bolting for the cafe front window.

Just as she reached it, the main door to the shop burst open and Gar came running in, his dark hair wet with sweat.

"Hey, sis!" he exclaimed, his words tripping over themselves. "Guess what? They found a body out by the falls!"

Great. The season was just getting started and we already had our first slip and fall. This wouldn't be good for business.

"Ugh," said Hope. "When will these tourists learn the rocks there are signposted 'No Climbing' for a reason?"

"Not this one!" said Gar, excited. "This one was an animal attack!"

Both Hope and I snapped to attention immediately.

"What?" I said.

"Yep," Gar replied. "I heard that whoever it was had their throat ripped open and their chest torn apart."

I swallowed the lump that made its way into my throat. I clutched at the pink stone jewel I wore around my neck, the one my mother had given me for luck on the night she disappeared. I was overtaken by a sense of dread like I had never felt before. I sank back against the counter, hardly able to register the patrons that were suddenly rushing from the shop and running in the direction of the wailing sirens.

The Girl with the Good Magic:
Chapter Two

I locked the shop door with a sigh after the last customer had exited. I could feel the slight buzz between my eyes that indicated a potential migraine was on the way. "Great," I said to myself aloud. "Just what I don't need."

"What don't you need?" Hope's voice caused me to jump. I had forgotten she was still here and had just gone to the restroom.

"Migraine," I answered.

"I'll help you clean up. That way you can close sooner and get out of here."

Before I could pretend to protest she had already walked around behind the counter, picked up a bus bin and started clearing the tables of the few saucers and coffee cups that the patrons had not left at the counter.

"Thanks, but that's really not necessary. I'm sure you have some place to be."

"Nope. We haven't seen each other in months. We have so much to catch up on." She stopped what she was doing and wheeled around to face me. "Unless you're telling me to go because you *know* there is someplace I need to be! Am I destined to meet Him tonight?!"

I knew she was just yanking my chain, but I also knew that part of her was dead serious. Rather than answer I changed the subject.

"So why didn't you go up to the trails and see what was going on with the rest of the town?"

"Once you've seen one mangled body you've seen them all," she miffed.

I couldn't help but laugh. "Honestly, the rumor mill must have been working overtime with this one. God knows how Gar heard it before the official reports. I mean, c'mon…an animal attack?"

"Well," Hope said, turning to me, "you know what that really means, right?"

"What?"

Hope rolled her eyes dramatically. "Please, I've watched enough *Supernatural* to know that animals never attack and kill people in real life. It's always a cover-up for something really nefarious. Like vampires, werewolves or some other bloodthirsty creature."

"Yeah, right," I say. "This is Trinity Cove, not the Hellmouth."

"Not if you believe the stories we grew up with as children. Don't you ever wonder why all the parents in town would never let their kids play outside after the sun went down? And why we weren't allowed to go outside at all during certain times of the month?"

"Probably because this was pre-internet days when pervs weren't lurking online but rather were cruising around in white vans, snatching kids."

Just then my phone rang and I couldn't stifle a little moan as I looked at the caller ID. I picked up before it could go to voicemail.

"Hi, Aunt Viv," I said, looking over at Hope. "Yes, I'm fine. I'm still at the cafe. Hope is here with me, helping me close. We'll be heading out soon, and I'll call you when I'm on my way home." I paused, looking over at a smirking Hope. "Aunt Viv, it's literally a five-minute walk home. I don't need...yes, all right. I'll see you soon."

"Let me guess," said Hope, "she's freaked out by the animal attack."

"'Freaked' isn't the word. She's sending someone to pick us up and drive us home."

"I'm sure she got all the good dirt on what happened," said Hope. "For someone that no one really talks to in this town, your aunts seem to know all the good gossip."

It was true. My family kept to themselves, but still managed to be on top of everyone's business. While I didn't want to alarm Hope, if there was anything supernatural going on in the area, chances were my aunts had already sniffed it out. Maybe that was why they were so intent on my being escorted home. Had they made the same call with Gar? If anyone needed protecting it would be him. He was powerless. Men weren't born with the power of witches. At least that's what my mother had always said. They could acquire it in other, less pleasant ways, but she had declined to explain what exactly those ways were. Aunt Vivian always said it wasn't true and not to listen to her. Men belonged to another pocket of the supernatural, she had said. They couldn't cross over into the corners occupied by witches.

The knock at the door distracted me from the espresso machine I was wiping down. "Sorry, we're closed," I said into the air.

It was dark outside and I could only make out the form of the person standing on the other side of the locked door. Another knock, this time more determined. Hope was closer to the door and peered out the window.

"It's a cop," she said. "He's holding his badge up to the door."

"Geez. Aunt Viv has taken getting us a ride to the extreme."

Hope moved to answer the door, and just as it cracked open it hit me: the smell of earth and rotted flesh accompanied by a wave of dark magic that made my stomach reel.

"Hope no!" I shouted, but I knew it was already too late.

Before she could react, the thing standing outside had burst in. The force of the door swinging open threw Hope across the room and over two of the tables. She crashed to the floor, unconscious. The sight of my best friend being hurt like that filled me with a white hot rage. I reached deep inside myself and grabbed that rage. Calling it forward, it manifested itself in a ball of blue flame that I hurled at the creature even as it charged at me.

Even as the creature was struck in the chest by my power, my thoughts raced as I tried to identify just what was attacking us. It looked like a human, a large, solidly built male. But I knew that when it came to the supernatural, looks could be deceiving. Whatever it was, it was only wearing the skin of a man. Underneath it reeked of death and darkness.

I dove behind the counter, looking desperately for anything that I could use as a weapon. The fireball I threw probably surprised me more than it hurt my attacker. I'd never been able to manifest my magic like that before. I could levitate objects and charge other items with magic, but I'd never been able to create something like that out of thin air.

I was too afraid to risk a peek over the counter to see where the creature was or what it might be doing. But then I remembered Hope lying out there, helpless.

"Shit!" I was sitting with my back against the counter, and looking around, I saw the silver cake knife lying on the floor. Knowing my aunt, it was probably real silver. That was a plus for what I was about to do. Silver has certain innate properties that make it both ideal for absorbing the right kinds of magic and for being anathema to supernatural constructs. I had no idea what that blue fireball I threw was, but other than the initial contact it didn't seem to have done much to the creature.

I crawled to the far end of the counter and chanced a quick peek. Whatever that thing was, it was lumbering to the opposite end of the counter, where the cash register sat. I winced as it grabbed one end of the counter and ripped up half the bar, throwing wood, glass, register and granite counters toward the ceiling as it shuffled around, looking for me.

"Okay, so you're strong, but you don't seem very smart."

I crouched, circling around the front side of the counter, trying to sneak up behind it, cake knife at the ready. How did this thing even get into the cafe? My aunts' wards were top notch. Anything giving off the kind of dark magic this had boy was reeking of should have set them off, given me some kind of warning. That told me that maybe this thing wasn't a supernatural creature, but something that probably has a contained burst of magic inside it as a power source. It smelled dead, so that meant someone probably animated a corpse and sent it after me. That's big time mojo.

But I couldn't focus on that right now. That thing was definitely strong enough to kill me and Hope, and that wasn't happening on my watch.

I concentrate and focused my will on the knife I was carrying. As I approached the creature, the cake knife began to take on a blue tint, glowing with the magic I was forcing into it. Just as I reached the creature, I heard a small moan. Hope was starting to wake up and had begun to move around. The zombie immediately spun in her direction and realized I was standing right behind it. Faster than I would have expected a dead thing to move, it swept me up in its arms and immediately started to squeeze.

I screamed in pain and raised the knife over my head. Had to do this before it crushed my spine, and judging from the pressure it was expending, that would happen in a matter of seconds.

With a yell, I plunged the knife down and into the creature's exposed neck. The silver, augmented by what little magic I have, was enough to pierce the flesh. But more importantly, it created an opening in the skin, a vent to release the magic that was powering this monster. What I did was akin to cutting the gas line on a car, only on a far more dramatic scale.

The zombie dropped me and staggering backward as black steam hissed from his torn flesh. The magic that animated him was evaporating, and with it, so went the monster's corporeal form. It fell to its knees before falling face forward onto the ground. The scent of rotted flesh breaking down for a second time was beyond nauseating. I retched as the smell hit me and instinctively buried my face in my elbow to ward off the fetid stench.

I could hear Hope coming to, dragging herself up to a

sitting position. In the distance I could make out the sound of sirens getting closer. As much as I hated to do it, I needed to get rid of the body.

I looked at the decomposing mess before me and muttered a quick incendiary incantation that melted it to so much slag, and then caused even that molten goo to evaporate. By the time Hope was looking around and clearing her head, I had moved to her side, trying to comfort her.

"What the…?" she mumbled.

"Hey, take it easy. Help's on the way."

"What the hell was that?" she said, rubbing the back of her head.

"Some coked-out druggie. Barged in, messed up the place, looking to take what little cash I had on hand, then ran back out. He's gone now." Not a lie. Not exactly, at least.

"Jesus, Allie. Are you okay? Did he…?"

"No, no. I'm fine. I think all my screaming scared him off."

I returned one of the knocked-over chairs to its upright position and slowly helped Hope to her feet before gingerly seating her. A knock at the door got my attention and I turned just in time to see a police officer stepping through the ruined opening.

"Ma'am, we had a report of a disturbance here," the officer said, looking around. I saw one hand hovering near his holster, which made me more nervous than being attacked by a zombie for some reason. Plus, his reliance on his gun told me he was not a supe. Still, I keyed up some magic and had it at the ready just in case.

"It's okay now. Some guy just burst in here, knocked all my shit over trying to break into the cash register, then ran back out," I said, trying to defuse the situation.

I watched as the policeman turned his head to the side and said something into a communication piece attached to the shoulder strap of his bulletproof vest.

He then stepped over to Hope and examined her head.

"Don't move, ma'am. An ambulance is on the way to take a look at you," he said.

"I don't need that," Hope replied. "It's just a bump. I feel stupid just sitting here like this. But can you make sure my friend is okay?"

I looked at the police officer and read his badge. Hunter.

"I'm fine, Officer Hunter," I said. "Thank you for getting here so quickly. I think it was the sound of your sirens approaching that scared him off."

"Did you get a good look at him?" Officer Hunter said.

"No...it all happened so fast. He was big, dressed in some type of large jacket and a cap I think..." Careful here, I tell myself. Don't back yourself into a corner.

"Oh my God!" said Hope. "I just remembered. He had a badge that he flashed at me when I looked out the door!"

"What?" said Officer Hunter. "Are you sure?"

"Well, it all happened so fast," I interjected.

"Yes, but that's why I started to open the door to begin with," said Hope. "Remember, we thought it was someone your aunt had sent to pick us up. I started to open the door...and then...then it gets fuzzy. But I know for a fact he had a badge."

Officer Hunter was busy scribbling in a pocket notebook he had pulled out of his vest.

Before he could ask more questions, the ambulance pulled up to the street in front of the cafe.

"Oh, good," I said, looking at Hope. "You really should

have them check you over, as hard as you must have hit your head when he knocked you over."

"Yeah," she replied, rubbing the back of her skull. "As long as they don't try to cut my hair or anything. I'm not having my summer do messed with."

Officer Hunter smiled as the paramedics walked in with bags and stepped back to give them access to Hope. I watched as he strolled around the cafe looking at things, examining the broken counter and making more notes in his little book. Definitely not good.

"We're just going to take her in for a couple hours of observation," said one of the paramedics to Officer Hunter. "She seems fine, but you never know."

The fact that this particular medic was about six-two and solid muscle was probably the reason that Hope wasn't putting up a fight. If anything, she was gazing at the first responder dreamily and rubbing her head even more.

For once I was happy to see her man lust rear its ugly head. Maybe it would keep her from focusing too much on the details of what had just happened here.

"I'll call your parents," I said. "I'll have them meet you at the hospital."

I watched as the medics loaded her into the back of the ambulance before turning to the officer as he exited my busted-up coffee shop and bakery. I really wanted to follow my best friend and make sure she really was okay, but I had a more pressing conversation to have with my aunts.

"So," said the officer, "I think I have enough for now, but I may have some follow-up questions."

Of course you will, I think.

"And I really don't think you should be walking home if that was what you were planning," he added.

"How'd you know?"

"Your friend said your aunt was sending someone to pick you up. No need. I'll drop you off."

I opened my mouth to argue, but the look he gave me silenced all objections.

"Fine. Just let me lock up and grab my purse." This was going to be a long night.

The Girl with the Good Magic: Chapter Three

If there was one thing my aunts were known for, it would probably be scaring the beejeezus out of the town folk, but that would only be if you asked the town folk. But no, that's not it. It would be their southern hospitality when it came to making strangers feel welcome in their home. Because truth be known, only strangers would come and sit in their home.

The house was a sprawling custom-built contemporary in the style of the old Victorians that used to dot the landscapes of North Carolina before the age of the McMansion: two floors of gracious living plus a full basement that ran the entire length of the home. The main floor and the basement opened onto sprawling decks that overlooked a picturesque backyard of mature trees and a babbling creek.

The home was part of an enclave of homes that sat up a winding series of roads along the top of a ridge. They were known as "back deck homes" because they all commanded such beautiful views of the woods, and neighbors would often converse with one another in the evenings while enjoying a glass of wine, waiting for the grills heat up.

The fact that they enjoyed such peace and solitude while only a short forty-five-minute drive to a major city never ceased to amaze me. The fact that Trinity Cove itself was almost considered a suburb of the city was one of the perks that made living here tolerable. We were the only access point to Singing Falls, so all traffic flowed through us. The ridge where my aunts lived ran above the roads that circled around to the falls, so that meant for the most part I got to miss all the congestion moving through the main streets. Until I had to go in to work, that is.

So having said all that, it stands to reason my aunts would invite Officer Hunter in for some tea, and they weren't about to take no for an answer.

"Oh, I'm sure the officer has more...rounds to do or something," I tried.

"Actually I'm officially off the clock," he replied. "But I don't want to be a bother this late at night."

"Nonsense," replied Aunt Vivian. "I insist you come in for some tea. My sister just put on a fresh pot and it's the least we can do."

"Well..." He hesitated. "I have always wanted to see inside one of these houses."

"Well, that settles it then," said Aunt Viv, ushering him inside the door. "Come on in and I'll show you around."

Like most officers, he wore one of those ridiculous broad-rimmed hats. I'd always wondered what the purpose of those was other than to funnel rain into your car when they stopped you during a storm and leaned down to ask for your license and registration through your barely cracked window. Whatever its purpose, he was kind enough to remove it as he stepped through the entryway. His head immediately craned back as he took in the twenty-five-foot ceiling in the expansive great room. To his left, stairs ran up to the second floor, spilling into the exposed loft area. The great room opened directly into the massive kitchen, complete with sixteen feet of granite island in the middle of the space. Beyond that was a set of French doors that led out to the deck overlooking the woods.

"Wow," he said. "This is far more impressive on the inside than the outside would lead you to believe."

"Well don't just stand their gawking," Aunt Vivian said, "come on into the kitchen and get you a cup. It's a beautiful night. We can drink it on the deck."

She gave me a look that said *don't even think about ditching*, and smiled as we all walked into the kitchen where Aunt Lena was just removing a kettle from the large, six-burner gas stove. She had already taken out a selection of teas and had them lining the island.

"Pick whichever you like, dear," she said, waving a hand over the selection. She had also placed four cups on the island as well as some sugar, honey, and lemon.

"Oh, I have no idea what's good," replied Officer Hunter. "Why don't you surprise me?"

Aunt Lena's eye browns arched in surprise and she couldn't help but chuckle slightly to herself. "Oh, now that I can do."

I frowned at my aunt as I moved to pick out some tea. Aunt Lena was the more somber of my two aunts. Her face was almost always contorted in a frown or some other mask of disapproval, yet here she was playing hostess to someone she had most likely never laid eyes on before tonight. I looked questioningly at Aunt Vivian and she just smiled at me, her gray eyes dancing in the soft overhead lighting.

I just shook my head and picked out some Earl Grey for myself. Whatever my aunts were up to was between them. But I hoped they realized that the more time they wasted with this guy meant the more time was passing before I could tell them what happened at the coffee shop. Which meant any possibility of tracking the black magic that was capable of raising a dead man from his grave was slowly slipping away. Aunt Vivian took the officer by the arm and escorted him out onto the deck, remarking all the while about how beautiful the night was.

As soon as they were out of earshot, I whispered urgently to Aunt Lena.

"Aunt Lena! I don't know what is going on here, but I really, really need to talk to you and Aunt Vivian! Something really weird and scary just happened to me tonight!"

"Shhh!" she practically hissed, her perma-scowl returning at once. "We can chat later! Right now we have a guest to attend to." She suddenly smiled mischievously. "A rather handsome guest, wouldn't you say? Plus, I didn't see a ring on his finger."

I actually felt myself blush at her comment. Dear Goddess, please tell me this isn't why they are doing this? Are my two aunts actually trying to set me up with a town officer? Suddenly I wanted to set my cup back on the counter and bolt for the stairs and the safety of my room. Aunt Lena must have sensed what I was thinking because she fixed me with a look that said, "I'll turn you to stone if you take one step out of this kitchen."

I sighed. Fine. The sooner this charade was over with, the faster I could get down to real business with the aunts. I turned on my heel, gave my aunt one last look over my shoulder, then walked out to the deck.

There was a large gas grill against the rails opposite the doors. Beside that there was a large six-person dining table covered by an even larger umbrella decorated with an array of hanging lights. Walking past that, I came to an intimate seating area bathed by warm, flickering outdoor candles. Aunt Vivian and Officer Hunter were sitting there talking quietly.

"So," I heard Aunt Vivian say as I sat down in a chair opposite the two of them, "you were just about to tell me your name. Unless you want us to remain so formal with you."

"Oh, no, ma'am," he replied. "My name is Cody. Cody Hunter."

Of course it was. I'm thankful that the flickering light hid my eye roll.

"Well what a beautiful name. So strong and manly," my aunt added. "Don't you think so, Allie?"

Jesus.

"I guess," I replied. "If you're a regular on a CW show."

I smirked, confident that my aunt wouldn't catch the reference, but equally confident that the good officer would. Before either of them could say anything, Aunt Lena came up beside us carrying a tray with a few more mugs arranged on top. She handed one to Aunt Vivian and another to Cody Hunter before settling down on a small loveseat next to us.

"Lena," said Aunt Vivian, "this polite young officer's name is Cody. Cody Hunter."

"Really?" said Aunt Lena. "Are you related to the Hunters over on Simmons Lane, or the Hunters of Trinity Drive?"

"Trinity Drive," Officer Hunter replied. "My family has been in this area for several generations."

"Oh, we are quite familiar with your family," said Aunt Lena, sitting back. "Drink your tea while it's hot, dear."

He smiled and raised the cup to his lips, blowing lightly

across the surface of the liquid before sipping gingerly. "Wow, that's really good." He took another sip, this one a little bigger.

"So I'm surprised that you and Allie don't know one another from school," said Aunt Vivian. "Were you in the same classes?"

"Honestly I don't remember, Aunt Vivian," I said.

"Oh, I remember you," said Cody. "You were a grade ahead of me and ran with a different crowd. We had an economics class together but that was it."

Great. I barely remember Economics, let alone who was in the class with me. Despite myself, I glanced at him a little closer and searched my memories. Nope. He was not bad-looking to be honest; his square cut jawline and brown eyes matched his name. But I certainly didn't remember him from school. Despite his assertion that I ran with a crowd, nothing could have been further from the truth. Other than Hope, I despised being around other teenagers.

"Interesting. Allie had a knack for keeping to herself. That could explain why she is still lacking in the social graces to this day," said Aunt Vivian. It was almost as if she were reading my mind. Hell, for all I knew she probably was.

"So where's Gar?" I asked, trying to steer the conversation away.

"He's in his room playing video games or doing whatever it is that young men his age like to do," said Aunt Lena. "Don't you go bothering him now; you just sit right here with the grown-ups and talk to this handsome young man."

I could feel my cheeks burn as Cody's eyes wandered my way. I immediately began drinking my tea, turning my body slightly away from his gaze.

"Oh, that's okay," said Cody. "I'm sure Allie has other

things on her mind than sitting here chatting with me. I mean, why should tonight be any different from any other time we've run across each other?"

I immediately spun around. "You mean the one class we had in high school four years ago?"

"No, no," he said, holding up a hand. "That's not what I meant. I come into your coffee shop almost daily. I see you around town quite a bit actually."

"Stalk much?" I didn't mean it; it slipped out before I could edit the thought.

"All right, that's enough," said Aunt Vivian. Her voice has taken on a slightly different edge, one that Cody wouldn't recognize but I did.

"I think I should be going," said Cody, moving to sit his cup on the small coffee table in front of him.

"Nonsense," said Aunt Vivian.

Now I was really annoyed. It would serve them right if I just got up and went to my room without telling them what happened. Let them figure out there's a rogue witch somewhere in town raising the dead.

"Finish your tea first and then you can be on your way if you'd like," said Aunt Vivian, her voice becoming just a little more singsong.

Cody obeyed, lifting the cup to his lips and taking in a couple of large gulps. That was when I noticed his movements. He was a little sluggish and off-kilter, an almost imperceptible sway settling into his shoulders as he placed the now empty cup down. I glanced again at Aunt Lena and notice her lips were moving. She seemed to be speaking, or at least mouthing words silently to herself.

Oh no. She wouldn't dare! She was casting, working some type of spell on Cody! She must have drugged his tea as well. That would explain his sudden lack of coordination.

"So that was some nasty business with the animal attack that everyone was talking about today," said Aunt Vivian casually. "Were you out on that call? It must have been so scary."

"Oh, ma'am," Cody started, "I'm not really allowed to talk about official business…"

"Oh, come now," my aunt continued. "This isn't business if it's just among friends. I mean, Allie here is your friend, and she is my niece. I'm sure neither of us want to see anything bad happen to her; so all I'm asking is that, if you know there is anything bad happening around here, you could tell us so we can protect ourselves, right?"

I glared at Aunt Vivian, but bite my tongue. Part of me wanted to see how this played out.

"Well…I guess that's true," said Cody, his words beginning to slur ever so slightly.

I glanced over at Aunt Lena. Her lips were moving at an even faster clip now. Her eyes had gone ghostly and gray under the strain of the magic she was pulling.

"Cody." Aunt Vivian leaned in. "Was there a body found at Singing Falls today?"

"Yes."

"Was it a fall from the rocks? An accidental death?"

"No."

"Was it an animal attack?"

Cody hesitated, his eyelids at half mast. "I…don't know."

Aunt Vivian looked at her sister briefly and then continued. "What do you mean? Surely the coroner has some idea."

"It looked like an animal did it, but there isn't anything in these parts that would do that to a body."

"Explain," said Aunt Vivian.

"The throat was torn open, so bad that most of the neck was missing. The head was hanging on by a strip of skin. The spine and larynx was tossed aside next to the body. The chest was mangled, but not by teeth. It looked like the ribcage had been split open by hand...or claws. The heart was missing, but other than that, the body had not been chewed at or eaten."

I clamped a hand over my mouth as I felt a wave of nausea hit me.

"Were samples taken from the body?" Vivian asked.

"Oh yeah. We found some weird hairs around the neck wound. They also took tissue samples and blood from around the body just in case some of it came from whatever did it. Working theory is it was a bear attack. One must have wandered down from the high country. At least that's what we are supposed to tell everyone."

"What's the unofficial theory?"

"No one will come right out and say it, but everyone is whispering that maybe *they* are back. You know, the werewolves."

I gasped audibly and Aunt Vivian shot me a look. I knew not to speak aloud; it can break the delicate spell Aunt Lena was weaving. I let my eyes apologize before my aunt continued with Cody.

"Cody, you have been so helpful. I want you to do one last thing for me. As soon as the reports come in from the coroner and the lab, would you be a dear and bring them to us here at the house?"

Cody frowned, but then nodded in agreement.

"And Cody, as soon as you do that, you will forget all about having done so. You will also forget that this conversation ever happened. We had tea, made small talk, and you enjoyed your time with us and my niece. That's all, okay?"

"Okie dokie," he replied cheerfully.

Aunt Lena leaned back, cutting off whatever spell she had cast. Aunt Vivian snapped her finger sharply in front of Cody's face and he was instantly aware and back to being his normal self.

"Oh wow," he said, looking at his watch, "where'd the time go? Thank you ladies for such a wonderful evening and that tea...I definitely need to pick some of that up. But I need to be going. Busy day tomorrow."

We all rose and thanked the young officer for his help and walked him to the door. He nodded again, placing the wide-brimmed hat back on his head, and headed down the drive to his car.

I turned to my aunts after shutting the door and couldn't control my excitement.

"Holy shit!" I exclaimed before I could stop myself. "When are you guys going to teach me the good stuff like that?"

"Allie!" said Aunt Lena. "Language!"

Grab your copy...
vinci-books.com/goodmagic

About the Author

M.J. Caan is an avid reader and writer of all things science fiction and fantasy. Author of multiple science fiction and paranormal fantasy series, M.J. likes to think that there is still magic out there in the world. Even if it's only between the pages of a great book.